no better time

The union has called a meeting tonight.
So many workers
are coming
there is not a single hall big enough
to hold us all
so we split ourselves between
Cooper Union and the Lyceum,
Beethoven and Astoria Halls.
Speakers have been scheduled
translators booked
I only hope
our pleas will not be met
with more of the same:

> *wait*
> *have patience.*

The thing is
there is no better time
for a general strike.
The shops are slammed with orders
the speedups are unbearable.
Even if the bosses bring in scabs
they will never meet their contracts
unless they negotiate with the union.

The thing is
I have already been on strike
for eleven weeks
I gave up
my dream
to fight for these girls
if they are not ready now
to fight,
then when
will they ever be?

OTHER BOOKS YOU MAY ENJOY

AUDACITY

AUDACITY

Melanie Crowder

speak

SPEAK
An imprint of Penguin Random House LLC
375 Hudson Street
New York, New York 10014

First published in the United States of America by Philomel Books,
an imprint of Penguin Group (USA) LLC, 2015
Published by Speak, an imprint of Penguin Random House LLC, 2016

THE LIBRARY OF CONGRESS HAS CATALOGED THE PHILOMEL BOOKS EDITION AS FOLLOWS:
Crowder, Melanie.
Audacity / Melanie Crowder.
pages cm
Summary: "A historical fiction novel in verse detailing the life of Clara Lemlich and her struggle for women's labor rights in the early 20th century in New York."—Provided by publisher.
Includes bibliographical references.
1.Lemlich, Clara, 1886–1982—Juvenile fiction. 2. Women in the labor movement—New York (state)—New York—Juvenile ficition. [1. Novels in verse. 2. Lemlich, Clara, 1886–1982— Fiction. 3. Labor movement—Fiction. 4. Immigrants—Fiction. 5. Russian Americans—Fiction. 6. Jews—United States—Fiction. 7. New York (N.Y.)—History—1898–1951—Fiction.] I. Title.
Pz7.5.C78Au 2015   2014018466

Speak ISBN 978-0-14-751249-9

10 9 8 7 6 5 4 3 2

for my grandmothers, Doris and Jo

AUTHOR'S NOTE

This book is a work of fiction loosely based on the early life of Clara Lemlich Shavelson. While most of the events in this story are true to history, in the instances where no record or conflicting records remain, the essence of Clara's spirit and historical accounts of her contemporaries were used to fill in the gaps. Some details have been altered to fit the form, and scenes imagined where the historical record is silent.

It has been an honor to imagine my way into Clara's small but mighty footsteps.

"Audacity—that was all I had. Audacity!"

—Clara Lemlich

tinder

1903

clouds

Over the gray plain of the sea
winds are gathering the storm-clouds

Words
float like wayward clouds
in the air
in my mind.

Now his wing the wave

     Wait—
or was it,

Now the wave his wing caresses

I dip a hand
into my apron pocket
unfold a square of paper
against my palm,
hunch my shoulder,
hide it from view.

     Ah,

yes.

Now his wing the wave caresses,
now he rises like an arrow
cleaving clouds
and

The poem is ripped
from my hand
and the air,

where only wayward clouds
had been,
is full of shouting,
accusations
a hand raised in anger
        ready to strike—

                the world slows
        in the second before
        pain blooms
        in my jaw;
                a second
        to hope
        the poem is
                        safe
in my mind
where fists
    and fury
cannot shake it free.

ordinary

Just because I am
small-boned
and short,
brown-haired
and brown-eyed,
just because I look

common
as a wren
meek
as a robin

that does not mean
what is inside me is also

common
as a wren
meek
as a robin.

Everything
I wish for
is strange
aberrant
even wrong in this place
but I know
I cannot be the only one
blanketing her bright feathers
hooding her sharp eyes
hiding
in plain sight.

My life
          so far

has been ordinary
simple
small

but I cannot shake the feeling
that inside this little body
something stronger
is nesting
waiting
for a chance
to flex her talons
snap her wings
         taut
and glide
far away
from here.

words

Mama says,
Sweep the floor, Clara,
like a good girl.

But a packed-dirt floor
is impossible
to clean.

Scratch, scratch
like a chicken picking grain from grit
I chase the dirt outside
where a thick-boned horse
pulls a rattling cart down the wide road,
his tail switching
side to side
flicking the flies
from his backside as he passes
the goose yard
the stonemason's shed
the tailor's shop.
(where if I can steal
an hour
I can earn a *kopeck*
or two
sewing buttonholes)

In the market,
where the Russian peasants
sell their goods,
a kopeck buys me
a scrap of paper
inscribed with stout
Cyrillic script:

a verb
translated
conjugated.

I set aside the broom,
run a dusting cloth
over the shelves
closest to the window.

The smell of spring
wanders in
on a wayward gust
of wind.

Across the street from Mama's store
the school is full of children,
blond heads bent
over lines of prose
primers held open
like *siddurs*,
like prayer books.

A handful of Russian words
float across the street,
mingle in the dust
my broom throws
into the air.

I pause,
do not even breathe,
my whole body

straining

to catch the sounds.

I turn the new words
            over and over
in my head
on my tongue
until they are mine,
            over and over
as I wipe the windows down
restock the shelves
fetch a bucket of coal
from the shed.

By the time Mama retires to the kitchen
to prepare dinner,
the school is shuttered
and empty,
the Russian girls
in their pleated brown dresses
and stiff little hats
have slung their satchels
over their shoulders
and skipped home.

In the handful of minutes
before Mama calls for me
I duck behind the house
follow the paths
the red deer stamped
into the ground,
into the woods.

I walk slowly,
clouds pinking
as the light
sinks
through the trees.

Every few steps I stoop
to pick up a feather
a coarse-veined leaf
a small
burnished stone.

Thrushes trill and tattle from the brush;
today
I have words of my own
to trade
for their song.

home

We live at the frayed edge
of our *shtetl*
between rows of straw-thatched homes
and the forest
where low-lying ferns
tickle the ankles of
slender trees.

I was born here
in a home split
between two families
our half split in half again
to make room for Mama's grocery store.
       (which means we are not so poor
       as some,
       that we can give a little
       to others)

We take care
of our own
here, in the Pale of Settlement
in the Russian Empire
hemmed in on all sides
by restrictions
   regulations
by people who only wish
to be rid of us.

a broken wing

Mama has released me from the store
                    from my chores
and the afternoon
is mine.

The ice in the streams is breaking up,
pale green spears
crocus buds
peek out of lifeless swaths
of meadow grasses.
I leave the path
dip a cloth in the stream
duck under the low-flying branches
of a pine tree
where a wooden box
rests against marbled bark.

I lift the roof
peer inside;
a winter wren
opens her beak
in a halfhearted hiss.

> *A few more weeks,*
>   I whisper,
> *and the splint can come off.*

The hiss gives way
to feeble cheeping.
I drop a beetle
a pair of dead moths
beside her,
settle a layer of brown grass

over her feathers
for warmth.

Hers is not the first wing
I have mended
but still I worry
what if,
when she is finally offered
a solid perch
a view of the sky,
what if she lifts her wings
only to find the air
                         still
cannot hold her?

work

Like all the other boys in our shtetl,
my brothers Marcus, Nathan
          and little Benjamin
study *Torah*.
Like Papa,
it will be their life's work
not farming or teaching
building or banking
but praying;
studying the holy ways.

Like all the other girls in our shtetl,
I am being trained in
obedience
hard work
a biddable spirit;
all the virtues
a good wife needs.

How can I tell Mama
who toils
          sunup
to sundown
to be a good mother
          a good wife
that this life
          (her life)
is not enough for me,
that I dream instead
of words
          ideas
a life that stretches far beyond
the bounds of this shtetl?

According to Papa,
a well-educated girl need know no more
than how to sign her name,
read the women's prayer book,
do a few simple sums,
write a letter to the parents
of her betrothed.

Mama says,
*Fifteen is not too young
to be thinking of such things.*

But to me
that word

[wife]

is barred and barbed
threatening
to hold me down
when all I want
is to stretch my wings
   to ride the fickle currents
beyond the reach
of any cage.

not one bit

Miriam says I can borrow
her father's copy of *The Cossacks*
if I teach her to sing *Kalinka*.

I am not supposed to know the words
to Russian songs—
even silly ones
about little pine trees.

So we hide
behind a *kalyna* bush
and I bruise my palms
beating the rhythm slowly
then faster and faster
while she rolls
shushing syllables
around in her mouth
like a hot gulp of broth.
The rhythm gallops
out of control
and we are left
giggling
gasping for breath
before we begin
all over
again.

> At the end of it
> I hold Tolstoy in my hands.

Back home,
I tuck the book
beneath my shawl.

A lie
in the shape
of pointy corners
hard edges
against my skin.
A lie I have become
all too comfortable
living with.
A lie
I cannot live without.

Kneeling beside the kitchen stove,
I stretch out my hands
as if to warm them
by the banked fire.

      (they only quiver
      a little)

When Mama looks away
I slip the book
under the stove
under the meat pan.

Hanna said
she will trade a book of short stories
by Ivan Turgenev
if I teach the song to her tomorrow.

I do not mind
a scratchy throat,
sore palms for a day or two.

I do not mind one bit.

yarid

Twice a week
I walk with Mama
to the market in the center of town
to buy fresh goods
for the store.
She wraps a scarf around her head
settles a basket
in the crook of her arm,
strides from stall to stall
stepping around the leavings
of horses, goats
and milking cows.
Her voice cuts across the clamor
of clucking chickens
and squealing pigs,
above the babble
of peasants pushing carts
pushing a sale
on anyone
who will listen.

Though Mama would never say
she regrets her life
I can see in the confident
cast of her voice
on market day
she relishes
                    this
her one
place
of power.

The cold crop
of vegetables
are stringy, the hens stingy
with their laying
but spring is here;
the air around the market quivers
with the white-knuckled grip
of peasants grasping
to last a few more weeks
when starvation
fades to the shadows
for a few
sun-kissed months.

While Mama barters with a man
unloading a wagon
of canned goods from Kiev,
I lift a corner of my scarf
to cover my nose
to block the stench of so many animals
crammed into one space.

With a glance over my shoulder
and a sidle between stalls,
I make my way to the wool cart,
greet Anushka
in Russian
in a quiet undertone;
I conduct a trade of my own.

Behind the cover
of our huddled shoulders
she unfolds a page
flowing with words

like water
rippling
over hummocks
and small boulders:
           a poem.
A *whole* poem for me today.

Anushka whispers,
I scribble translations
in the margin,
hand over my kopeck
with a smile.

If it would not draw
too much attention
I would kiss her on the cheek
for this lovely
lovely gift.

secrets

Miriam's family has a farm
with chickens and goats
and a big draft horse
with delicate
white-tufted hooves.

If I stand on my tiptoes
wrap my arms
around his neck
if I stretch—
reach for my
fingertips
they still do not touch.

Sometimes
when I am done
with all my chores
at the grocery store
Mama lets me walk
down the dirt road to the farm.

Miriam leads the gelding
out into the fallow pasture
we take turns
hefting each other up
onto his high, wide back.

He trots obligingly
though he has already worked a long day
clearing fields,
      dragging
the heavy plow behind.

I whisper secrets
into his mane,
things I tell
no one else.

shul

The Yiddish word for synagogue
means school.
There is little we hold
in greater esteem
than learning
       (of course,
         just for men)
than study
       (of course,
         just the holy books).

I learned to read
and write Yiddish
by lingering
in the kitchen to polish
       the *samovar*
       the *kiddush* cup
       the candlesticks,
          to wipe
       the grease
       from the cast-iron stove
when the tutor came
for my brothers.

When I was young I wished
I had been born a boy
so I could study, too.
Now I wish instead
that I was born into a family
where a girl's yearning for stories
              for learning
              for understanding
is not driven out

like a foreign body
excised from the skin.

In our home
only Yiddish is permitted.
No Russian.
Papa forbids it.
It is the only way he has
to protest.

> *But, Papa,*
> *   I say,*
> *all there is to learn, all those books*
> *—philosophy, medicine, history—*
> *they are all in Russian!*

> *Enough, Clara,*
> *   Mama says.*
> *You are a young woman now.*
> *It is enough.*

> *   Papa says,*
> *Politics are not for girls.*

In an idle conversation, he hears
                the shouts of the mob
in a simple poem he sees
                the blood frenzy
                the way a word
                can twist
                slur
                cut.

I know this,
yet I could not hold back
my need to learn
                    things
            if I tried.

At the kitchen table
covered with prayer books
Marcus leans in
nodding
smug
Benjamin flushes
flinching away
from the same
tired fight.

I want to yell
            rail
            rant
but I know
it will do me
no good.

I learned long ago
to douse these angry flames
to make the coals burn
low
but steady.

lies

In this life,
        lies
take the shape of words
printed on ivory paper
stitched into neat bundles
wrapped in linen casings.

It has taken years
of stolen moments
whispered conversations
borrowed books stashed
like contraband—
                years of lies
but I am nearly fluent in Russian.

When life offers me
something
beyond
                this

I am ready.

preparation

Friday mornings
the store floods
with women.
They come from all over the shtetl
clutching the kopecks
they have saved all week
to buy something extra for *Shabbos* dinner
    a jar of honey
    a potato to thicken the soup
    a tin of oil to crisp the fish.

Mama bolts the door
when the last of her customers has gone.

We are both tired
from scrubbing the house
the night before.
        Tomorrow,
        we can rest.

I follow Mama through the curtain
at the back
into the kitchen.

She hums
as she stokes the fire,
the furrows in her brow
smoothing,
her hands settling
into the rhythm
of ritual.
She cinches her apron
around her round waist;

through a long, deep breath
a thread of song
escapes her lips.

I crack an egg
knead the dough
set it aside
to rise
in a warm nook
above the stove.
I clear the table
spread our best cloth
over pocked wood
arrange the dishes
          the kiddush cup
          the candlesticks,
snip a bouquet of twigs
from the bushes
surrounding the house.

I walk to meet Benjamin and Nathan
they run through the meadow
a brace of trout dangling
from their bobbing
fishing poles.
I clean the fish myself
behind the coal shed
so Mama's sacred space
will not be disturbed by the fuss
                         and rush
of carefree boys.

When I was young
I fished for slippery trout in the stream

on Friday afternoons, too.
I had a pole of my own;
I ran through the meadow
        free as a bird
swinging a string of fish
behind me

before all this business
of being a woman
took over.

dance

Hanna and I
would never have been friends
if we did not both
love to dance.
Though we are confined
to the same shtetl,
her family is infinitely wealthier
than mine.
Hanna was sent away to school
when she was a girl.
She knew three languages
by the time she returned to us.

But she was generous
in her friendships
not too great
to dance
with the daughter
of a poor scholar
and an even poorer farmer.

Hanna shares her books
Miriam shares the debates
she and her father wage
well into the night
over politics
the coming revolution
the attacks
against the Jews.

Miriam and Hanna and I
meet in the woods on Saturdays
to dance under the trees

to trace the pattern of
budding branches
drawing shadows against the sky.
When the weather warms
we will dangle our feet in streams filled
with long grasses
lying down
like ribbons rippling in the water.

We go our separate ways
when the sun begins to fade;

at night
I wait until the house is silent,
light a stubby candle
creep out of bed
my heart high
in my throat
my breath short
and quick.
I tuck into a quiet corner
read my Tolstoy
in the yawning shadows.

herbs

In the meadow
behind the shtetl
pale shoots have begun to sprout
from the skeletons
of wild sage bushes.

       I worry a downy leaf
       between my fingers.

When Nathan was only three,
his lungs filled
his throat constricted
his pale face sweated with fever.
I sat at the foot of his bed
while the doctor
dug through his kit of instruments
listened to my brother's wheezing breath
spoke in hushed
foreboding tones.

I had not yet seen a book
on physiology
pathology
or medicine
but the Russian folk songs
I had learned in secret
held instructions—
       which herb to seek
       for a cough
       which bark to boil
       for a fever
       which berry to crush
       to soothe the skin.

I searched the meadow
for sage
wild thyme
and mint
to make a compress
for Nathan's chest,
gathered the splayed white petals
of the kalyna flower
dried them in the shade
brewed an infusion
to quiet his cough.

I do not know
if it was the doctor
and his instruments
Papa's prayers
or my poultices
that pulled Nathan through
the worst of it,
but my fingers
have never forgotten that feeling
of being so very
necessary.

Though the sickness
has shown no sign of returning,
Nathan has always been pale.
Pink splotches bloom
high on his cheeks;
Mama tests the heat of his brow
every morning
just in case

thyme and mint and sage grow
in the kitchen garden,

bunches of dried herbs
hang from the attic rafters
just in case

my book of medicine
hides with the rest
just in case.

lost

I heft the bundle of clothes
ready for washing
in the river
swing it over my shoulder,
step slowly through
the hastily thawing ground
on the path past the outhouse;
careful not to slip,
tip the bundle
into the mud.

The door to the kitchen
bangs open
Papa fills the frame,
his beard blunt
as an ax
my books raised high
over his head
in a hand
shaking with rage.

My hands rise up
on their own,
the laundry tumbles
out of its neat bundle,
wet shadows spreading
on threadbare cloth
like bloodstains on a bound wound.

I run inside.

    Please, Papa,
    please!

The kitchen stove
squeals
as he pries open the door,
                           hurls
my books

one

        by

                one

into the fire.

I sink to my knees
in front of the flames—

                        all those words

                        singe
                        and flare

                                                        lost

my lungs seize
my eyes water
my throat burns
from the ache of breathing in
all those lost words.

Marcus stands behind Papa
arms crossed over his chest.
Benjamin,
whose eyes

always seem to hold
a measure of fright,
watches from the kitchen table
clutching his books
tight.

Mama says,
Wash the clothes, Clara,
like a good girl.

faith

Frustration swells
seeps out of me,
rises again until my head pounds
                    my teeth grind
with the effort of holding it in.

I am like the macaw
chained to the gypsy caravan
that rumbles through the shtetl
each summer,
out of place
dropping bright feathers
one at a time
molting
withering
in an unfriendly climate.

How can I ever be more
than just someone's daughter
                    wife
                    mother
if I cannot study
if I cannot learn
if I am not permitted to have
even one book?

I know Papa thinks
this fire in me
stands against
the faith he holds
so dearly

but I see our faith
as the thing
that lit this fire in me
to begin with.

letters

I may be unschooled
but I will not
be ignorant.

The widow
at the end of the street
wants to mail a letter to her son
who sailed for America.
She cannot write
but I can
and she is not the only one
who will pay
for such a service.

I will buy my own books now
find a new hiding place
up the ladder
in a corner of the attic
under a beam.
No one will find my Tolstoy
              my Gorky
              my Turgenev there.

service

The talk in the women's balcony
has a furious
mournful edge to it.
Mama's face is pinched,
every time I lean in
to listen
she clucks in disapproval.

> *Sit up straight,*
> *she says,*
> *we have no need*
> *for idle gossip.*

Mama loves the whispers
that fill the minutes
before service begins
so I know this story is something
she especially
wants to keep from me.

I wait through the prayers
and the ritual
the men act out below,
peek between links
in the screen
that hide us
from view,
my feet dancing
beneath my skirt
with impatience.

When at last the service is done
I rush outside,
catch Miriam's arm.

Tell me.

Her eyes are wide
her mouth twists to the side
in an almost-smile

> *Clara—*
> *you have not heard?*
> *No, of course your mother*
> *would keep such news*
> *from you.*
>
> *Hanna's cousin Ruth*
> *wanted to study at the university*
> *in Kiev*
> *but of course,*
> *the only Jewish girls*
> *allowed in the city*
> *are prostitutes.*

I nod
yes, I know this
have I not rolled this problem around
in my own head
like a stone
tossed along the riverbed
bumping against boulders
all the way to the sea?

> *She did it,*
> Miriam says.
> *She got a prostitute's badge*
> *moved into the city*
> *so she could go to university.*

Cold wraps around my arms
encircles my wrists
like shackles.
The breath in my lungs
is thin as wisps of clouds
whipping across the pale sun.

I pull my shawl tighter
around my shoulders
open my mouth
to speak

but I have no words

     for this.

Pesach

Tonight we remember
when the angel of death
passed over the homes
of the faithful.

I think
       as I watch the light from the candles
       flicker and dance
       to the breath
       taken in
       and measured back out
       in the recitation of the *Haggadah*
if it took decades
for the slaves to be freed from Egypt
how long
must I wait?

I do not need bitter herbs
bites of potato dipped
in the tears of my ancestors
to imagine a life
devoid of choice,

where my own destiny
is gripped in the fists
of others.

monsters

A boy was killed today
in Kishinev.
A Russian boy;
a Christian.

The Russian newspaper
says he was murdered by Jews
planning to use his blood
in the preparation of *matzo*.
                    Monsters,
            it calls us.

The printed words begin to rattle,
then blur before my eyes.

Papa snatches the paper
from my fingers
I jump back
my hands clenched
my jaw set.
I flinch
in spite of myself,
cry out
when his open hand
crashes
into my cheek.

I hold a bucket
of rusted, bent nails,
hand him one after another.

He hammers boards
over every window.
Our home shudders
with the force
of his blows.

Papa's anger
lingers
like the smoke of animal fat
filling the air,
thick
oily
burning my throat.

pogrom

When the church bells tolled
in the distance
                    I asked God,
        Please, let it be
        only a sign
        of their mourning

but no,
it was the priest
calling his flock
to pick up their pitchforks
            their hammers
            their torches
in holy vengeance.

Mama bursts in, her hands pulling,
lifting us up and out
even as the words fly
soft
as moth-winged
whispers from her lips:

        Go!

Why is she whispering?

        Go to the woods—
        hide!

Mama grabs little Benjamin
thrusts his stick arms
into a woolen coat
winds a scarf around his head.

Scatter,
         she says,
stay hidden
until I call you home.

Benjamin is trying to be brave
but his hands are shaking,
the sleeves of his jacket fluttering
like the wings
of a stunned bird.
I loop my arm in his,
pull him with me.

        Where is Papa?
           Marcus asks.

Mama herds us toward the door,
arms flapping like a farmwife
shooing the goats from the laundry line.

Marcus pushes back

        Where is Papa?

Mama makes a sound
low in her throat

        Gone to protect
        the scrolls,
        and NO—

she grabs his arm
pulls him back

you will not
go with him.
Mama thrusts packets of food
wrapped in cloth
into our hands,
drops hasty kisses on our heads
pushes us out the door.
Marcus and Nathan
touch the *mezuzah*
kiss their fingers as they leave.
I cannot.
My hands are full.

Mama—
what about you?

Her face closes like the trap
on a spring-loaded snare

Go,
she says

and shuts the door.

I grab Benjamin's hand
and run.
Our footfalls
pound like hammers,
Benjamin's rasping breath
loud as a bucket of nails
dashed to the ground.

We follow the deer path
into the trees.

The air is silent,
the birds
quiet,
the woods filled
with children
shivering
waiting
for it all to end.

We run
through the marsh
into the coarse grass.
The kalyna bush
at the edge
of the meadow
is thick,
bursting with new
green leaves.
I tuck Benjamin
beneath the branches
burrow in
beside him.

Marcus and Nathan
are nowhere to be seen
already hidden away
out of sight.

My mind
races;
I try
to pace
my breath
slow
as I can

though
my lungs

are slow
to listen.

hours

The sun hides, too;
little more than a white glare
behind thin clouds
revealing nothing
of the minutes
or hours
as they pass

if they pass
at all.

dusk

I hate this hiding
in the shadows
      hate
the way
my mind
dances
to the rancid
rhythm
of fear.

      Is Mama safe?
      What is all that smoke?
      How close will they come
            this time?

The light fades
from the sky;
one by one
the forest fills
with mothers
calling their little ones
out.

The pent-up nerves
jangling,
fed up
cries rise up
to fill
the woods
with questions
and wails
and whys:

I want to go home.

Why are we hiding?

Where is Tata?

Mamele, is that our home burning?

Benjamin wiggles out
from under the branches,
runs to Mama,
whose arms are piled high
with blankets.

Tonight
we will sleep
in the woods
with the night crawlers
and the wolves
and the soft-throated owls.

sunrise

The sun
cannot find a clear path
in the morning;
the smoke
makes the air
blush
with shame.

The bloody sky
is the only sign
of the screaming
begging
shouted prayers,
of all that burned
the night before.

It is not the first time
the peasants have attacked us
as a salve for their pain.
But it is the first time
I wonder,

       if a bloodthirsty mob
       is coming
       for each of us
       someday
       no matter what we do
       or do not do,

is there any point
at all
in fear?

quiet

When Mama calls us home
at last
at the end
of our second day in the woods
my fingers
are stiff as kindling sticks
my bones
creak like an old woman's

but my mind
is quiet
certain.

I have never known
what kind of girl I am
not at home in this shtetl
not at home in this family
not at home in this life.

But I know one thing now:
I will not be
the pheasant
quivering
hiding
from the hunter
who crushes the slender reeds
to flush out
his prey.

      I will never
            cower
      like this
      again.

a favor

The thing that brings us together
will always be stronger
than that which pulls us apart.

Suffering
is the great unifier
of our people.

In the morning, a small crowd gathers
sets off down the road to Kishinev
builders hefting tools
the doctor with his kit
and the *rabbi,*
whose back is bent low
by the weight
of lifetimes
of prayers.

I tug on Papa's sleeve

> *Let me go,*
> > *I say,*
> *I want to help.*

> *Daughter,*
> > *he says,*
> *can you stitch together*
> *their wounds*
> *their hearts*
> *their lives?*

> *We do the only thing*
> *we can*
> *for them.*

We pray.

In the bleak morning light,
everything I struggle
so hard
to learn
seems frail
foolish, even.
What good is an education
if it cannot heal
the gash
bleeding out
before my eyes?

By noon,
the carpenters
bricklayers
blacksmiths
have all returned.

No one is interested in repair,
in rebuilding.
Anyone lucky enough to be alive
is leaving.

Forty-nine people were murdered.
Hundreds more beaten
bloody,
thousands of homes
destroyed.

The police did nothing.
Why should they?
The mob was doing them a favor,
killing Jews.

unblinking

I lie
unblinking
in the dark.

Is it wrong
that I am angry

    —so angry
    the chill in my bones
    trickles to my fingertips
    until they pulse
    with a frost-born fire—

at a father
who would brave an angry mob
to save the books he holds dear
but casts the ones I cherish
into the fire?

Is it wrong
that I am grateful

    —so grateful
    the air in my lungs flutters
    like a scrap of paper
    let loose in the wind—

that they did not come
just a little farther
down the road,
that they spent their rage
in that shtetl
and not this one?

leaving

We are leaving,
> *Papa says,*
as soon as we can save the money.
We will cross the continent
to a seaport
find a steamship
that will carry us
across the Atlantic Ocean
into exile
again.

Tears leak from Mama's eyes
staining the worn fabric of her apron
pressed against her mouth
with the palm of her hand

but she does not argue.

Hanna is gone
the following day.
The wealthy families scatter
like snowflakes
in a strong wind
to any country that will have them,
gone to America
> Australia
> the holy land.

The rest of us hoard our kopecks
until we can buy our way out
of this place that has turned
against us.

We wait
like rabbits
sniffing at the edge of our burrows
testing the air
never sure if it is safe
to go out.

The yarid is quiet,
business is done
in quick
curt exchanges.

I do not visit the wool cart.

Much as I long
for another poem,
I cannot look Anushka
in the face
anymore.

test

I return to the forest
only once

lift the winter wren from her box
hold her tight to my chest
so she will not struggle.
I snip the splint
lift it away
stretch her wing wide.

I close the roof
of the nesting box
settle the bird on the branch beside it.

I turn away
hurry along the path toward home—
I cannot bear to wait
           to watch her test her wings,
          to see
                if she will fly
                or fall.

packing

Miriam and her family left today;
just like that
all the laughter
has gone out of this place.
The farm is still
the stalls empty,
ragweed clambers eagerly
over untended furrows.

By the time Mama closes up her store
there are hardly any Jews
left in town
to buy from her
            anyway.

I wonder,
who will the Russians blame
for their problems
once we are all
gone?

Papa and Marcus
wrap the holy books
in linen.
Mama digs through Benjamin's sack
trading toys for stockings
an extra pair of pants
a wool vest.

        It takes an eternity to choose
        only one book
        to bring with me.

I wrap first
my underclothes
then my dresses
then my winter coat
around a slim volume of poetry
tuck the bundle
into a sack
I can carry over my shoulder
when we leave here.

The rest I leave in the attic.
They have books in America.
They have schools in America
                    even
                    (I hear)
                    for Jewish girls.

Hope lives in an uncomfortable
infrequently visited space
beneath my ribs.
I am wicked to think it
              —I know—
but I wonder
if on the other side
of all this anger
                    violence
                    uprooting
if America
is just the place
for me.

goodbye

We ride to the city
in the back of a wagon
on top of a load of
potatoes.

I sit,
watching the road behind us
my feet dangling
in the dusty air.
The grasses sway
in the warm winds
seedpods flutter
waving goodbye.
Barn swallows flit between buildings,
perch on swaying cattails,
cheeping and twittering
as if this were a peaceful
lovely shtetl.

I try to fix this picture
in my mind
so when I remember this place
from the other side of the world,
I have something
other than terror
to think of.

spark

1904–1905

mirrored

The train station is full of people like us
carrying their whole lives
on their backs
like a great army
of snails.

Looking into their faces
is like looking into a mirror:
the same deep furrows
shadowed eyes
pinched lips
staring back at me.

The space above the tracks shimmers
with heat.
There was no leisure
in summer's arrival
this year; its hot breath
blows grit in our faces.
The air carries a sharp smell,
something I cannot place.

Mama's eyes are glassy,
constantly blinking
as if she spent the whole day
looking into the wind.

the German Empire

The guards check our papers
as we cross into this territory
and out of that one

their words
so familiar
      (as if our tongue and theirs
      were not-so-distant cousins)
their meaning
so clear.
      (how could it not be
      with all the pointing
      and scowling
      and stomping?)

We are shuttled into a brick building
separated, men from women
stripped down
hosed off
dusted with powders
that burn my nostrils
      my throat
      my eyes.

Even with our clothes
on our backs again,
even in the heat
Mama shivers.
I grip her hand
grit my teeth
to keep my chin
from wobbling.

I will not let fear
find purchase
on my skin
again.

They wave us past
once we are clean
once they are sure
        we are not staying
        only passing through
once they are sure
        we understand
        what all those pistols will be used for
        if we veer from the route through
        and quickly out
        of their country.

I fold my papers
tuck them close to my skin
let out a long full breath
once we have left the soldiers
behind us.

murmuration

The whistle blows
    loud
as a cast of raptors
shrieking.

      I never heard such a thing!

In one instant
the flock of travelers
heft their bags
jostle
to first one door
      then the next.

          Marcus follows close behind Papa,
          Mama herds Nathan
             before her,
               I grab Benjamin's hand
                   hold tight.

        This line spills into that,
        everyone vying for space
               trying
        to stay together
           like a cloud of starlings
          swarming over a wheat field,

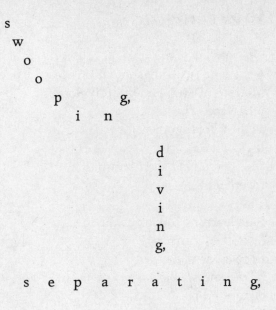

s
w
o
o
p
i n
g,

d
i
v
i
n
g,

s e p a r a t i n g,

re
group
ing,

settling.

look away

On board at last,
we wedge our things under our seats.
Mothers clasp their children close
pinch their lips tight
as if by holding in
their words
they could hold their families
together.

I am learning to look away
from the weariness
hopelessness
helplessness
all around me,
though I cannot ignore
the way uncertainty
like a heavy cloud
rises from the unwashed skin
of hundreds of bodies
packed together.
I lift the corner of my coat
to cover my nose
lean into the window
wait for the great engines
to carry me away,
or at least to stir the air
a little.

Benjamin's legs dangle
inches above the ground.
When the train jolts into motion
I tuck him under my arm
            under my wing
to keep him from slipping.

I watch
through smoke-stained windows
as we chug past
tidy crops
lonely towns
shadowed woods.
I wonder if Miriam
or Hanna
rode these same tired tracks.
I hope
they landed
somewhere safe.

My brothers open a book
prop it between them
one half perched on Marcus's leg
the other on Nathan's
as if it is the most natural thing
in the world.

Jealousy sweats
like a clammy fever.
If I pull my own book
out of my bag
Papa will toss it out the window
of the moving train
like a piece of trash.

whirligig

Hours later,
when the train
screeches to a stop
  to unload a tower of crates
  onto the platform,
  to trade the empty coal bins
  for full ones

my head bobs atop my neck
wooden and wooly
as if I were one of Benjamin's toys
with wheels
painted eyes
and whirligig arms
haplessly dragged
across the floor
knocked into chair legs
and doorposts
and discarded shoes
along the way.

stars

The train never tires
though I lose count
of the hours
we have spent on board.

When I wake
                fitfully
during the night
it feels as if the whole world
is passing before me
with only the unblinking stars
as my witness.

Hamburg

Finally
the train stops for good.

We have only a moment
on the still
solid earth
before we are led like cattle
through the stocks
scrubbed
deloused
discharged onto a steamer
that chugs
up the Elbe River.

It is as if
they could not get us off their land
fast enough.

The boat sends ripples in its wake
fanning out like a flock
of geese in formation,
nipping at the wavelets
rolling across the water.
We curve through the heart of
this green land
on a murky river
reluctant to share its secrets.
Bells toll in high towers
as we glide under scalloped bridges
in the rippling shadows cast
by crenellated walls.

When the mouth of the river opens
spills into the North Sea
we cling to anything
not buckling
or bending
in the face
of the vaulting waves.

None of us
have found our balance
yet.

strangers

I thought the sea
would smell brisk
                 fresh
full of adventure
but the salt in the air
stings my eyes
and the stench
burns my nostrils.

I make my way to the rail
drinking in
the slim gray expanse
where England rests
just above the waves,
awaiting our arrival.

Our third day aboard the steamer
when the sun climbs
to its highest point in the sky
we sidle up to a floating dock;
by the time we are shuttled
to the poorhouse
in the bowels
of the city
the moon has taken its place.

I do not understand a single word
the officials speak.
English is no cousin
to Yiddish
or Russian.

We truly are strangers
in this place.

gone

I am tired of the same tinned fish
and stale matzo—
kosher food we carried
on our backs
from the shelves of Mama's store—
and I wish now
that I had brought all my books.

We wait
   through the last dregs of summer
   and into the first cool sips of autumn
   for a steamship
   to carry us across the ocean.
We wait
   in a poorhouse thick with fleas.

       (I think I could forget
       all the places that itch
       if I had something
       to read)

An angry hum
rattles the room;
word has just arrived.
The trial for the murders
in Kishinev is over.
Hardly a witness appeared to testify, so
hardly a punishment is handed down.

My tongue turns sour
in my mouth.
Of course
there were no witnesses.

We are all either dead
or gone.

I go out
during the day
just to breathe
unshared air
to shake the despair
that falls like dust
from the rafters
and settles on my skin,
          the despair of a people
too well acquainted with suffering
to believe
something better
waits for them
on the other side of the ocean.

thoughts

The pogrom is fresh
in our minds
in our dreams.

Not one of us is sleeping through the night.

If Papa's thoughts
are black
as the sludge
coughing
from the smokestacks
at the docks
then Mama's
are gray as the thousands of layers,
cloud upon cloud upon cloud,
that never lift from the English sky.

> There is no privacy
> in the poorhouse,
> no space
> for my own thoughts.

But when I go out
beyond the endless rows of cots
        (jammed
        together
        like so many
        matchsticks
        in a box)
beyond the walls
I find that the very air
is thrumming with ideas

whispers
on wing beats
                    pumping
                            pumping
                                    pumping.

listen

Every day
I make my escape

     from Papa and Marcus *davening*
          Benjamin and Nathan bickering
          Mama worrying
                  when
          will we leave this awful place?

     from the poorhouse
          where the noise
          of so many people
          packed together
               clangs against the brick walls
               clamoring for the high windows
               clamoring for a way out.

I walk to the seaport
watch the boats come in
     and go out
     grand crafts with billowing sails
     stout steamships belching smoke
wish for the day
when our ship will come.

          I feel like a falcon
          tethered
          tied down
          while an eager wind
          beckons.

On the streets
I listen to the speakers

rallying the onlookers
to their cause
  anarchists
  fundamentalists
  royalists.

I do not agree
with everything I hear
but I am enthralled
with this place

where the streets do not clog with mud
in the autumn rains

where elegant houses
line neatly cobbled streets

where students of every creed
learn together

where I am not banished from the city
for being a Jew

where ideas
                words
are free
to anyone who wants them.

ideas

Socialism
        (the man on the soapbox explains)
means no one is better than anyone else
everyone shares

the same rights
the same protection
the same opportunity

no matter their station
no matter their religion
no matter their gender.

At last!
I have a name for the ideas in my head.

He gives me pamphlets
invites me to lectures
asks questions
I do not yet
have answers for.

At last!
There is work for my mind in England.

December 3, 1904

After months of waiting,

                                          finally

our boat comes.
Three stout masts
and two funnels
thrust up from a deck
skirted by rooms
for those who can pay
for a glimpse
of the sky.

We watch
as fine ladies follow a trail of porters
carrying trunks to their cabins,
our breath forming frosty clouds
of impatience
in the air.

Then the second class
boards, all order
and dignity
without so much as a glance
for us
who wait on the docks
perched on the bulging sacks
that hold everything we own,
the drear
that never lifts from the air
wetting our hair
seeping through our skin
into our bones.

When steerage is called
a flurry of movement
spins around us:
families call to each other
link arms,
the little ones cry
hold tight against the push
and pull
that could pry
them apart
as the great horde
of people
are herded
toward the cargo hold.

It does not seem like we will all fit into that

       hole

in the ship's deck
but the line keeps moving;
the ship swallows
us all.

There is no adventure
in steerage
in the misery
that waits for us
beneath.
I know why I
will send myself

into that filthy darkness
but I wonder
        as I watch
        the travel-weary faces
        march past
what private horrors
        improbable hopes
spur them on.

We shuffle forward
until Mama and Papa, my brothers and I
step onto the gangplank
over the gray, foaming water,
onto the sea-washed decks.
The crewmen,
cheeks chapped by rough winds,
their eyes fixed
in a squint,
point us down the steep ladder.

In the hold below
lit only by greasy portholes
there is nothing to break
the press of unwashed bodies, to move
the tepid,
stale
air.

I find myself
wishing for the fog
longing for the chill.

We claim our bunks:
metal slabs

two high
two wide

each covered with a burlap mattress
a life preserver for a pillow
a small pail—for eating?—
not unlike
the one Miriam used to scatter
the chicken feed.

Papa and Mama and little Benjamin
take one bunk
Marcus and Nathan
settle into another.
I sling my sack onto a top bunk
crawl up after it
turn my face to the tarred planks
that separate us
from the ice-cold water.

The mattress crinkles beneath me
filling the air with a pungent,
briny scent.
                    What kind of hay
                    smells like the sea?

I pick at a loose seam
pull out a strand of the brittle stuffing.
Seaweed.

The heat at the back of my eyes
            disperses
the ball in my throat
            dissolves
I pull my book of poems

from the bottom of my sack
hide it in the crook
between my knees and shoulders
whisper each line
in time
to the gently rocking boat.

Nicco

A young woman and her tiny baby boy
share the mattress next to mine.

She holds a hand to her chest
              and says,
     Isabella.

She touches
a single finger
to the boy's downy cheek.
A smile warms her voice:

     Nicco.

She sings to him
in a language
that sounds
like a songbird.
I wonder why she is here
in the belly of this boat
all alone.

The engines roar
the ship blasts its great horn
groans away
from the docks.

I stay below.
I have no desire to watch
the old world
fading
as we pull away from its shores.

It is only when we are far
from the docks
and the supper line
has begun to form in front of giant
simmering vats
full of gristly stew
that Mama's search
through our bundles
becomes frantic.

> *Where is the tinned fish*
> *and the matzo?*
> *Where is all the food*
> *we brought from home?*

We scramble to help
counting bundles
upending piles of travel-worn clothing
but it is no use
we must have left it behind
at the poorhouse
or in the confusion
at the docks.

Without the food from Mama's store
keeping kosher on this ship
is impossible.

Before Papa has the chance
to utter an edict
I will not follow
I grab my pail

      and say,

We all know
America does not take in
the sick.
A ten-day fast
would make us all seem weak
and sickly.

Mama's arm lifts to cover
Nathan's shoulders.

I say,
If we do not eat
we will be sent back.

I reach a hand to Benjamin
he looks between Mama
and Papa
and back at my outstretched hand
his stomach grumbles
as it is always doing.
Papa sighs
Mama passes a pail
to each of us.
Benjamin places his small hand
in mine,
together
as a family
we walk to the end of the line.

at sea

It is the strangest thing—
belowdecks
      I know it is the sea
         tossing us

        side   to side

sometimes rocking
sometimes pitching

but to climb into the open air
and see nothing

                        for miles

but rolling gray waves
as if a legion of beasts
skimmed the water in perfect formation
just below the surface
         —to see the force
     that holds us
         at its mercy
is a thing
I cannot find words to express.

Though the wind
lashes my skin
like shattered icicles,
as often as I can
I walk the section of the upper deck
permitted to us in steerage,

stumbling in the open air
like a newborn goat
on spindly legs
not to be trusted,
                    giggling
at my own clumsiness.

If Hanna and Miriam were with me
we would dance
on the pitching deck
holding hands
and singing.

I dance anyway
all by myself
and send my song
into the wind.

sons

Mama cannot resist
the cooing baby
        (even if he is
        Italian)
she clucks over little Nicco
while I duck behind her shoulder
then pop out again
to see his eyes flash wide
to hear his laughter
bubble to the surface
again and again and again.

In such close quarters
everyone pretends
not to see
        hear
        smell
everyone else.
But Nicco
has our neighbors
in the bunks around us
leaning in
smiling, even.

Papa turns his back
gathers his boys
around him
opens the Book of Job for study.
He does not have to say a word
for his opinion
to be heard.

I wonder if Papa ever looked at me
the way Isabella
          with her musical words
          and small, happy smile
looks at Nicco.

Or is that kind of feeling
reserved
only for sons?

breathe

The weather has turned.

Storms lash the waves
                    and us in them
across the roiling face of the water.

I thought there could not be a smell worse
than fish and brine,
unbathed skin and rotting seaweed.
But the storm has chased those
made sick by the sea
belowdecks.

One thousand souls
share the same foul space.
The air burns with the reek of vomit;
the floors
are slick with filth.
I have to use the toilet
but I make myself wait
out the storm.
I cannot risk a trip
to the toilets
where the sickest among us
swarm in their misery.

We all know
about the island of tears
that waits for us
at the end
of this endless ocean
the place where the sick are culled
turned back
turned away.

I will not go back
        —not after the possibility of a life
        filled with meaning
        has been dangled before me.

I will not allow anyone
to send me back.

I tuck my face into the crook of my arm
breathe the smell
of my own skin,
try to think of something

        —anything
        else.

morning

Our fifth day at sea
dawns clear
and terribly cold.
The ocean is calm as bathwater
lapping at the edges of the sky.

Out here
in the middle
of the sea
the sun does not even look
like the sun.
With nothing to frame it
     tree branches
     thatched roofs
     church towers
it is just a waxy brightness
sliding oh so slowly
across the sky
as if there were no need
to mark the time passing
at all.

fighting

Little Nicco is sick.
His face is red with fever, his fists balled,

      fighting.

The ship's surgeon visited,
only his eyes visible
above the cloth
pressed to his nose and mouth.
      (whether to keep infection
      at bay
      or just the stench
      of this place
      I cannot say)

He listened to the boy's heart
and lungs
felt for the faint pulse
inspected mouth and eyes.

I have no herbs here;
all my grand ideas
my secret studies
could not save anyone
in Kishinev
cannot help Nicco
now.

I pick up Isabella's pail
and wait
for over an hour in line.
The cook sloshes a ladleful
of gray gruel inside
without meeting my eyes.

I lift the pail onto our bunk,
set it beside Isabella.

Mama pulls Nathan
away from the sick boy
lifts her hand
to check his brow
settles the round bulk of her body
between her son
and the sickness.

She has no more room
in her bruised heart
for sorrow.

I wrap my shawl around my shoulders,
climb up the ladder
onto the deck.

    Are our prayers
    even heard out here
    in the middle of the fickle sea?

I turn my face into the wind
until I cannot hear
Nicco's weakening cries
until I cannot see
Isabella's panicked eyes
anymore.

sinking

He died in the middle of the night.

No one slept
through the sound
of Isabella's grief.

I climbed out of my bunk
squeezed next to
Benjamin.

In the morning
the ship's carpenter rips apart
an apple crate
nails a few of the planks
back together.

Isabella lays her baby inside
the tiny coffin,
turns away
while they hammer the lid
shut.
The captain says a prayer
lowers the narrow pine box
onto the waves.

The box was lined with sand,
holes bored in the sides
so it would sink
swiftly,
but even so, the pale glimmer
of the little coffin in the water
seems to follow us as far as it can
before sinking
into the deep.

shiva

I do not know how Isabella's people
honor the dead.

Our rules can bend
and flex
when our family is at risk
but Papa would not approve
of me altering the old ways
for this.

Still,
in the time we have left
I will bring Isabella water for washing
and food,
set a bowl of water
at the end of our bunk
as if she were one of us,
sitting shiva
for the only family
she had left.

The captain says
we will arrive in America in a few days.

I wonder
if the old ways
will have any place
in this new world.

close enough

I spotted a tern
flying over the ship today,
a chevron of white
against a perfectly
blue sky.
The arctic air gusting off the sea
tossed it about;
it flapped
haphazard,
wayward,
fighting against the wind.

Until that moment,
I never wondered
where all the birds had gone.
They flew beside
and above us
for a few miles
off the English shoreline:
skuas,
cormorants,
and ungainly big-mouthed pelicans.
But in the middle of the Atlantic
with no coast to break the endless water
the sky was empty.

To see one now
means we are close to shore.
One day,
maybe two,
and we are there.
                  So close
a seabird could fly out and back
in a day.

But not close enough
for Nicco.

land

We are belowdecks
when shouts and cheers
erupt above.

We scramble for the stairs
like a crowd fleeing
a burning building
everyone rushing
to the front of the boat
for a glimpse of the thin gray line
on the horizon.

My brothers hoot and dance
Papa prays
Mama's eyes are bright
her fingers lift to cover trembling lips.

As the ship pulls into the harbor
the spires of giant buildings
thrust into the clouds.
Everyone is pointing
            gasping
            marveling
at the wonder
of a city built toward the sky.

The port teems with traffic:
tugboats, ferries
and small fishing craft
rock in the waves we send in all directions.

The mother of the exiles
holds her torch aloft
greeting us in the water.
The clouds break apart
and for a moment
pure
clean
rays of sunshine
reach through the heavens
to dance across my cheeks.

Here,
at last,
a welcome.

Even for us.

lines

We hurry to gather our things,
impatient
to feel the earth
beneath us again.

A quarantine doctor
nods in approval
as the first-class passengers disembark
    (he barely looks them over)
and then the second class, too.

For us?
More lines.
One to get on the ferry
one to get off the ferry.
A line
snaking through
the warehouse
  s o   l o n g
it wraps like a curving tail
around the back.
A line
that ends
in a verdict:
stay
or go?

I turn
to where Isabella waits,
slumped
defeated.

Inconsolable
and insane
are easily mistaken
one for the other.
The thought of her
being turned around,
sent back over that fitful ocean
again
is unbearable.

I rush back to where she stands,
ignoring Mama's cries,
I wipe her face
prop her up
pinch some life
into her cheeks
so after everything
at the very least
she has a chance to begin again
in this new place.

medical inspection

White veined walls
naked lightbulbs
humming
cold metal
instruments
pinching

eyes staring
squinting
roving
up and down
fingers poking
prodding

goose bumps ripple along my bare skin
shame blooms
scarlet
on my cheeks.

powerless

Always more lines.

Waiting for this inspection
         that interview
         a stamp on those papers.

Mama and I pass through the inspection
and soon Papa, Marcus and Benjamin join us.

But where is Nathan?

I have never seen Papa
so powerless
as when Mama began to question
then wail
then beat her fists against
his chest.

       Where is my son?

       There is nothing wrong
       with his lungs,
               Mama insists.
       He is perfectly healthy.

Papa speaks
in a tender voice
I have never heard
him use.

       The doctor said
       they will keep him here

for a few weeks
and return him to us
when the infection clears.

And if it does not?
         Mama asks

but Papa only shakes his head
closes his hands over her fists.

The high ceilings echo
with cries.
We are not the only family
culled
the strong from the weak.

A moment ago
relief pulsed through my body

now it has turned
into icy trails of guilt.

blind

We wait
on the whims
of officials
who have forgotten
how to smile.

Papá swears
to be faithful to this new country
to forsake the land we left behind.
He whispers a promise of his own,
an echo of King David's words:

> If I turn traitor
> to this, our new home
> may my right hand wither
> from the arm I now raise.

This moment
that should have felt
like coming home
has left us stumbling
and starting at any noise,
casting around
as if we have lost
our sight
unsure how to move forward
while leaving one of our own
behind.

aliens

I do not know what I expected
when we finally stepped off the ferry
onto American soil
as landed immigrants
    legal aliens.
Maybe that the sun would shine
a little brighter
        that someone
would share in our sigh
        of relief.

We heft our sacks
over our shoulders.
It is just as Mama always says:

> When the Messiah comes,
> keep working.

New York City

We step away from the pier
a cheerless
muddled bunch.
We follow the line of immigrants
into a bank of dark buildings
that rise like cliffs
all around us.

                    I have never seen
                    a city so frantic
                    so full.

The squawk of gulls
the clang of buoys fade
before the rumble
of pushcarts on cobbled streets,
footsteps like droning
drumbeats.

The briny sea gives way
to the smell
of wet newsprint
    roasted peanuts
    coffee brewing
        in a street-side café
    piles of garbage spoiling
        in the alleys.
The streets are a tangle of trolleys,
motorcars, horse-drawn carriages
and an unending spool
of people going briskly
about their business.

After the third or fourth turn
I cannot see where we left
the ocean behind.
How can you tell north from south
                    east from west
in a place
with no horizon?

> *Benjamin,*
>   I say,
>   trying to coax a smile
>   onto his mournful face,
> *can you count the windows*
> *going up?*
>
> *How can a tower*
> *of steel and glass*
> *fly so high?*

Before long,
he is a hummingbird
impossibly small
unable to stop
zooming
                              this way

          and that

gawking
puzzling
marveling.

Before long,
our footsteps drag

and stumble,
I lose count
of the city blocks
we have walked.
I switch my sack from my left arm
to my right
and then,
after another dozen blocks,
onto my head,
steady it with both hands
to keep it safe
from the crowd of people
pushing past.

My skirt is impossibly grimy
from months of travel
I do not bother to lift it away
from the sloshing,
spitting puddles.

To our right
arched pillars rise out of the East River
stout cables lash the Brooklyn Bridge
to the earth.
Men in fine suits
children
workers
saunter across
as if such majesty
were their birthright.

something we understand

We step a little quicker
when the babble around us
becomes a clamor
we understand.

The third person Papa asks
points us to a building
with a vacant sign in the window.
The landlord leads us
up gaslit stairways
flanked by walls
covered in peeling paper
and cracked molding.
He unlocks the door
to a dim apartment
we can rent for ten dollars a month,
three tiny rooms
for all six of us.
          (when Nathan
          joins us, that is)

But we have sturdy wood planks
beneath our feet
two windows to the street
where you can see
a scrap of blue
if you press your cheek
against the glass,
tilt your head skyward.

The toilet is indoors!
          (though we have to share it
          with the three other families
          on our floor)

But the smell—
it almost makes me wish
the thing was outside after all.

The first thing Mama does
in our new
            (if well-worn) apartment
is unwrap the Shabbos candlesticks
place them in the center
of the table.

The first thing Papa does
is unwrap the mezuzahs
that traveled all those months,
safe in his breast pocket,
and nail them to the doorposts.

I hang a blanket over the
air shaft window
to keep the Polish woman next door
from watching everything we do.

Marcus unpacks his books
recites Torah
as if nothing
has changed.

night

In the shtetl
I could escape to the woods
when I needed a moment
for myself.
In this city
in this tenement
in this apartment,
private moments
are hard to come by.

Mama draws the curtains
over the windows to the street
Papa follows her into their room
and closes the door.

In the parlor
Marcus arranges pillows
Benjamin stretches out
      head on the sofa
      hips and feet propped up
      on a row of crates
a broad smile on his face
as if this were all
a grand adventure.

I have a bed to myself
little bigger than a crib
tucked beside the kitchen stove.
It is lucky I am so short!
And lucky, too,
this luxury of sleeping alone.

For once I am grateful
to be a girl
in this family.

When all is dark
and the noise of the city
has dimmed,
my mind opens
like a nighthawk's wings
gliding beneath the stars.

In the shtetl,
to speak the secret wishes
of my heart
would have been foolish.
Impossible, even.

But here
I think
        (I hope)
it is not so.

I test the air
with my softest whispers
to see if it can bear
the weight of my dreams:

        I will go to school to study.
        I will become a doctor.

stitches

In the sliver of daylight
beside the parlor window
Mama picks out my stitches
one at a time.
Every woman in our building
takes in piecework
to help pay the rent.
We borrow a pair of needles
        a wooden spool of thread
to practice.

    Again,
        Mama says.
    Smaller. Neater
    this time.

I grit my teeth.
Surgeons need still hands
for all those
small,
neat stitches.

If the way to my dreams must be laid
on a trail of tiny stitches
at least they leave a path
for me to follow.

I bend
over the scrap of linen
stretched taut
like a gypsy's tent between my fingers

and stitch,
   stitch,
   stitch.

gloom

Our first week in the city,
Mama goes out every day
asking for a job.
Papa and my brothers
go to shul
to pray
for Nathan.

I stay
in the apartment
in the tenement
jammed against the ones beside it
leaning toward the one behind it,
the one before it blocking all the light.

Until we have an income
we cannot afford luxuries
like oil for the lamps
so I take down the blanket
over the air shaft window
prop the door to the hallway open
so a little light
can find its way in
to the kitchen
while I wipe the coal stains
from the walls
scrub away the grime
the last tenants left behind.

I set the dishes for meat,
the spoon
the ladle
the knife

in the cupboard
across from the stove.
I arrange the dishes for milk,
the spoon
the whisk
the glasses
on the shelf above my bed.

In any extra hour
I can steal
for myself
I walk outside
under the pale winter sky.
Water towers perch like buzzards
on top of the buildings,
elevated trains
scatter dust and grime
block the sunlight
as they rumble past
casting blinking shadows—
an arpeggio of piano keys
playing on the streets below.

Children sell pretzels
and papers
men fill the cafés
and synagogues,
the noise of their debate
            their study
            their davening
spilling out onto the streets.

            I wonder,
            where are all the girls my age?

possibility

A woman with a baby on her hip
scoops coal into a dented pail
as I descend into the cellar.

We talk
as she scoops;
she waits,
talks some more
as I fill my pail, too.

She has the best news—
there is a school on Madison Street!

The moment my chores are finished
I walk across half of the East Side
to get there,
to the Jacob Gordon Free School.

                    [free]

I would happily
walk all day
for such
possibility.
I ask inside
just to be sure,
though I do not see any girls
in the classroom.

The director behind her desk
answers,

Yes, of course
all are welcome
free of charge

though there is something
she does not say
some pitying thing
in her eyes.

I memorize
the cross streets
sketch a picture
in my mind
of the buildings
leading the way there.

My feet skip across the sidewalk
all the way home
like a mallard glancing off the water
as he lifts,
gusting upward
into the sky.

Perhaps I will not have to work first
to earn my way
into school.
Once Mama finds a job
I could carve out time for classes
by waking up early
starting my chores
while the rest are still asleep.

I drag the washbasin
into the bedroom
so when Mama comes home
she can have a moment
to herself
to wash away the chill
            the grime
of a day on the city streets.
I fill the kettle
add a scoop of coals to the fire
fan the flames
until the water begins to murmur
                        then bubble
                            then burst.

sunlight

There is a small space
wide as a horse-drawn cart
between the building where we live
and the one behind it.

Just before noon,
before the sun has reached its highest point,
that space
fills with light
          and warmth.
The tenement empties
like sand spilling out of a broken jar.
The alley swarms with children
women bring their piecework
and sit, their faces tilted up
to catch the sun
as it filters through the
silted city air.

In under an hour, it is gone again
slipped past the edge of the next building
like an egg yolk
sliding out of the shell.

impossible

Mama comes home
at noon on Friday
to begin Shabbos preparations
with nothing to show
for five long days of looking.
There are so many immigrants
desperate for work;
a grocer who left her store behind
is of little interest
to anyone.

We need to buy food
and oil; pay rent
pay for seats at shul for the holy days.
      (at least for Papa and my brothers)

So Papa decides that on Monday
I will look for work
instead.

On this holy day
which should be restful
          thoughtful
          inspiring
the gloom
inside our apartment
seeps through my skin
weighing down
my limbs
pressing like an iron
filled with red-hot coals
against my chest.

School may be free
but how can I go
if I am to work all day long?

So much is different here
from our shtetl—
       language
       people
       work
       chaos
       progress.

But really,
nothing has changed.
We travel halfway around the world

                        and still
my dreams are impossible.

flame

1905–1907

sweatshop

After a morning meal
of hard bread
two eggs shared
between the five of us
Papa takes Marcus to shul
to pray
for Nathan.
I go looking for work.

I start at the school.
       I can speak, read, write
       two languages.
       Surely someone
       will pay for a tutor.
The director turns me away,
but kindly.
English is the only tongue of interest here.

Next I try the grocery stores.
They do not even tell me why
I am shooed away quickly
and not so kindly.

The day dawned bright
and clear;
now heavy clouds have moved in,
a drizzle
darkens the cobbles
beneath my feet.

I stop in a café
spend a penny
on a glass of milk

for lunch,
sip slowly
so my stomach thinks
it is enough.

Each day
the soup is thinner
our portions of bread smaller
Benjamin's rumbling stomach
louder.
Mama does not say it
but I think
we are near the end
of our coins.

In the shtetl
at least we had
a kitchen garden
community donations
to feed the hungry.
But here,
a garden is impossible
and no one has extra pennies
to give.

The waiter, at least
has a helpful tip

> he says,
> *There are always jobs*
> *at the garment shops*
> *for girls like you.*

I wonder
what that means

          (a girl like me)
but I follow his pointing arm
to the shops
up the street.

It is there I learn
my first English word:
     sweatshop

there is no Yiddish
or Russian translation
for the rows
and rows
of women
and girls
some of them younger than me
breathing air clogged with smoke
from the coal-burning stove,
shoulders hunched
sleep-starved eyes squinting
at the fabric before them
ears ringing
with the
          BANG BANG BANG
of the machines.

All those grim faces—
is that what the waiter saw in me?

I have to shout
to make myself heard
as I visit shop after shop after shop
asking for work.

I have to say
if I am looking for work
in a place like this
it must be true—
I am one of those
                desperate
grim-faced girls.

celebration

I am not the only girl looking for work.
I visit three shops
before one in a cellar
below a clothing store
ten blocks from where we live
has an opening for an apprentice
to a sub-subcontractor.
The workers
teenage girls like me
middle-aged women
a handful of men
cut, iron, stitch together
pattern pieces
of starched white cotton
into tapered blouses
called shirtwaists.

Starting tomorrow
I will work seven days a week
ten hours or more
each day.
I will earn six dollars
to bring home at the end of each week.
          (though I have to buy
          my own needle
          and thread)

Now that I have found work
I can begin English classes
at the free school in the evenings.

I buy a fat
salted pickle to celebrate

take tiny, ant-sized bites
so it lasts all the way home.

obedient

I should be happy
to bring home money
for my family
but I know now why
I found a job
so much faster than Mama.

The shops prefer to hire girls
who will work longer days
for less pay.

Have we not been told
all our lives
that a good girl
is obedient
biddable
meek?

All these good girls
marching to work before the sun rises
marching home again after it has set
balancing bundles of piecework
on their heads.

An army of girls
trained in silence.

I have never been
obedient
or
biddable
or
meek.

In this world
where I am made to be
something I am not,
small,
secret things
wither
inside of me.

lock

Slam
twist, click.

Locked inside
a brick box

bile rises
lungs pump

workers shuffle
to their stations.

Stools creak
heads bow

needles stabbing
bobbins banging
thread marching in

straight

steady

seams.

Breath settles
panic swallowed
footsteps click
stool creaks
my own head
bows down.

search

At the end of the day
the foreman unlocks the door.

The workers form a line,
their eyes fixed on the shard of sky
        just visible
        between two buildings
        almost touching,
their faces
empty
lips drawn
tight over gritted teeth.

One by one
the foreman
pats the workers down
roving over curves and creases
searching for scraps of fabric or thread or dignity
                that might find their way out
                of the shop.

                when it is my turn I cannot make
                myself take that last step forward
                so he comes at me and again I am
                only trying not to flinch not to cry
                out not to quiver not to fling those
                hands off curves and creases that
                have only ever known my own two

                                        hands

sleepless

night winds
wind through the streets
below
moaning
wailing
drawing down courses
                of tears
out of a starless sky

forbidden

My second English word
is written on placards
all over the shop.
It means

a rap on the knuckles
        if I talk
a clap on the back of the head
        if I laugh
a smack on the shoulder
        if I so much
        as hum.

            It seems everything
            is *forbidden*
            in this shop.

When I walk home through gaslit streets
after work
after two classes at the free school
Papa's anger is steaming
bubbling
like a kettle
left to boil over on the stove.

            He says,
            You were supposed to be home
            by seven o'clock.

            I say,
            I had English classes
            after work.

I forbid you
to attend classes at night,
             he says.

English is not Russian, Papa.
This is not the language of persecution
it is the language of our freedom.

             He shakes his head.
You will come home
after work
to help your mother
with the cleaning.

All my life
I have been told
a daughter can do no worse
than talk back to her father
but I am so *tired*
from the terribly dull
             terribly long day.
I smell
like that sweaty
stale room that trapped me inside
all day

and I cannot bear
that word
one more time.

         I worked ten hours
         for this family.
         I have earned an hour
         or two
         for myself.

I know better
but still
                    I say,
            You help her.

I brace myself
set my jaw against
the blow
I know
is coming
but still
my head whips back,
the sound of his hand
smacking my cheek
seems to come from somewhere
hollow
inside my head.

I know
he thinks
to break this thing in me
that insists
I think
for myself

but like a fledgling
thrust from the nest
it only makes me test the strength
of my own wings.

Sundays

Mama walks under bare branches
                  just beginning to sprout
                  young buds
to the pier
to call Nathan's name
across the water.

The ferry docks,
drops its latest crop
of immigrants
on these shores.
Mama begs a crewman
to deliver a letter
to Ellis Island.

He takes the paper
she presses into his hands
whether or not he understands
her pleas.

Mama believes he does as she asks
but I wonder
if her letters are not simply tossed
into the waves,
                lost
in a sea of tears.

truce

There is still no news of Nathan
so Papa and I have settled
on an uneasy truce.

The immigration documents
are in English
the quarantine officials
speak English.

Mama keeps the house
Papa takes my brothers to shul
to pray,
I work
I learn English.

We all do our part
to bring Nathan home.

mornings

I have become adept
at getting dressed
in the dark

feeling for the bend in my stockings
heel
then knee.
Buttoning,
lacing, cinching.
Twisting my frizzy hair up
into a coil
that will not unravel
no matter how late I work.

With my first few paychecks
and the pennies
from her piecework
Mama paid the rent
purchased food
covered a single wall in the parlor
with a creamy yellow paper
                —just the color of the sun rising
                through the window
                of her store in the shtetl—
with scrolls and blossoming vines
climbing toward the ceiling.

A boiled egg
a thick slice of unbuttered bread
out the door
stepping around the rats
that scrabble in the hallways,
down the stair.

My feet find the sidewalk
where the air is alive
with the sharp smell
of warm rain
on dusty cobbles,
where I cannot see
more than an arm's length in front of me
but I can hear
the brisk swishing of skirts
as thousands of girls
walk with me.

In the shtetl,
we woke with the cock's crow
with the sun rising,
turning the tips of the meadow grasses
into pure gold.

If I am honest,
I admit
that on some lonely,
sleep-hazed mornings
when I cannot see a thing
but the hulking shadows
black on black
of building
after crumbling building,
I long for that simple,
quiet place.

English class

I wash the dishes,
    the teacher says.

I wash the dishes,
    we repeat.

A dozen eggs, please,
    the teacher says.

A dozen eggs, please,
    we repeat.

Do you want starch in the collar?
    the teacher says.

Do you want starch in the collar?
    we repeat.

The classroom at the free school
is full of young women like me,
workers,
their hats tilted
at an angle
as they listen
to the teacher's words.
I am told
the men learn elsewhere,
learn different phrases
about work
and money
and business

words that will help them rise
beyond
this place.

Learning English
is no luxury
   no idle pastime
   no domestic exercise
for me.
Do they think none of us
wish to rise
too?

No matter,

I am accustomed to schooling myself
gathering words
like a squirrel
hoarding nuts.

break

Nathan's absence
seems to have taken years
from Mama.
White wings sprout
in her dark hair;
her hands grow rough
her fingers tilt to the side, cramped
from balancing the thimble
pinching the needle
pressing the darts into place.

Tonight,
she sets her piecework aside
to give her eyes
their day of rest.

The Shabbos candles are lit.
Soft smiles
murmured blessings
pass around the table
with the salt
      broiled fish
      golden brown
      braid of bread.

We do not voice
our worry.

We do not speak
about how tomorrow I will break
Shabbos, how I will be up
before dawn
like every other day
and go to work.

one of us

Our people have always
migrated
across borders
trying to find a place
that will tolerate our presence
for a time.
We flock together like geese
flying thousands of miles
only to nest at the same
small pond.

At evening service,
when I point out
the owner of the shop
where I work

       Mama says,
How lucky you are
to work for a man who knows
the teachings of the prophets.
A man who is one of us.

       I think
if a man drives his workers
like a slave master
what does it matter
over which holy book
he prays?

drapers

In the morning,
before work
has rounded the corners
ground down the edges
of my mind,

I study the shop
while the foreman's back is turned.
I know by now,
if I am to save money
for college
I will have to make a higher wage.

    I watch

the cutter
at the front
near the stairs
near the air to the street above
leaning over his stack of cloth
balancing a blade
long as his arm
slicing two dozen pattern pieces
at once.
At the very top of the long list
of things forbidden
in this shop
              is cigarettes.

But the cutter is a skilled
valuable worker
he pays no mind,
his ashes drifting

toward the scrap heap
daring the fibers
to burn.

      I watch

the pressers
lifting and lowering irons
that weigh as much as I
over and over
all day long.

      I watch

the drapers
lifting, pinning, cinching, snipping
stepping back
heads tilted to consider their creations
called up out of simple
unadorned cloth.
Shirtwaists come in all styles:
      pleated
      billowing
      finely embroidered.
Creativity
and deft fingers
to make small stitches
are rewarded.

I duck my head
as the foreman clicks to the dim
rear of the shop
where we

        [the less skilled
        much less valuable workers]
bend over our work
basting and trimming,
stitching bits of lace
and buttons
to finish the look.
When he is gone again
my fingers move
on their own

and I watch the drapers
at their work.

look around you

We are not in the shtetl
anymore.
We have traded the greens
and ambers and rich browns
of the fertile earth
for right angles
sidewalks
towers that scrape
the underbelly
of the sky.

What it is to be a Jew
is different here.
Those of us who work
say our prayers
thrice daily,
observe Shabbos
in our minds
and hearts
only.

Mama cooks and cleans all day
takes in piecework
in the evenings,
as if by working her fingers bare
she could stitch sutures over the gash
rending this family
apart.

We work until we cannot
anymore
and still
it is not enough.

No man here
has the luxury of studying Torah
instead of working
if he wants his children to eat.
All my hard work
goes to pay
for a way of life
that is impossible here.

I bite my tongue to keep
from calling down
my own father.

> *Look around you,*
>   *I long to say,*
> *next time you go to shul*
> *in the middle of the day.*
> *Do you see anyone there*
> *but the rabbi?*
>
> *If you want this family to eat,*
> *get a job*
>
> *and hold what is holy*
> *in your mind*
> *and heart*
>
> *like the rest of us.*

books

Nadia,
who sits next to me
while we hunch
over our stitches

      [day in
      day out]

tells me about the East Broadway branch
of the New York Public Library.

              She says,
        It is full of books
        for anyone
        to read.

Anyone?

I do not believe her.
I laugh outright
and the foreman
clicks across the room
to swat the back of my head.
When he is gone,
Nadia whispers directions.

        I make her repeat them
        three times.

At the end of the workday
after the foreman is done
checking our pockets
patting us down

to be sure we are not stealing
from the shop
he lets us outside,
where spring has sent
a last
fitful rainstorm
in farewell.

I walk beneath the skeleton
of the Manhattan Bridge
the sound of hammers and welding torches
echoing against the cobbles.
Out in the middle of the river
men work, suspended like tightrope walkers
above the river
piecing together a roadway
out of thin air.

On the outside
the library might be anything
       a bank
       a school
       a government building.

On the inside
it is as if someone
looked into my soul
fashioned the thing
I long for most.

I climb the steps, staring,
my mouth gaping open
like a landed fish.
Quiet study tables
fill the room.

The walls are lined
with shelves of

books   books   books   books   books
books   books   books   books   books
books   books   books   books   books
books   books   books   books   books
books   books   books   books   books
books   books   books   books   books
books   books   books   books   books
books   books   books   books   books
books   books   books   books   books
books   books   books   books   books
books   books   books   books   books
books   books   books   books   books

floor to ceiling.

It is as if my heart
leaps out of my chest
to strum
the spines,
thumb through
the pale,
hand-softened pages.

Most of the books
are in English
and I only know a few words
so far.
But I find an entire section
for the Russian novelists.

I will come here after work
after my English classes

when I can
         —a book for dessert
after the long, hard days.

surprise

Nathan has come home!

His lungs are clear
his cheeks round
and rosy
it seems that in the last few weeks
he has been fed
better than any of us.

Mama fusses
and clucks over him
Papa smiles broadly
to see his son
returned to him.
My brothers hurry
to rearrange the crates and pillows
make room for Nathan
on the couch.

I am happy
of course
that Nathan is home at last,
but I wonder how we will fit
another body
in this tiny apartment,
how my meager salary will feed
one more hungry mouth.

summer

Even the air blisters
in the heat.

In our building
and all along the street
people drag their mattresses
onto the fire escape
onto the sidewalk
onto the roof.
Indoors the air is
stifling;
it is impossible
to sleep.

The dawn hour is the coolest
but so little so
that I wonder
if I only imagine it.
With the summer sun comes light;
I can see the cobbles beneath me
as I walk to the shop
stepping over
and around
hundreds of fitfully
sleeping bodies.

My feet have grown, again
and my shoes pinch
my toes
with every step.
The money I give Mama
at the end of the week
is enough for rent

for flour, meat and potatoes
and a little oil for the lamps.
It is not enough
for new shoes.

I am lucky, even so.
The women who work
the sewing machines
carry them on their backs
to and from
the shops every day.

At eight o'clock
when the shop door closes
and locks,
we sweat
at the back of the workroom,
our throats dry
our faces blotched, red.
The pressers wield their irons
with a slam and a scream of steam
boiling up from the edges.

It is a near thing
guessing how many sips of water
I can take without needing the toilet
        (which is in the backyard
        behind the shop)
until the foreman unlocks the door
at lunch.

I spend my days dreaming
of the whirring blades
of a single fan,
an open window

to the street,
the impossible
giddy longing
for rain.

The air cannot find
this dark corner
in this maze
of a city.
How could it
when every building reaching
for the sky
steals a little more
from the breeze?

unchanged

The iceman came today
with his delivery.

It is all Mama can talk about—
the wonders of this city.

But life is unchanged for my brothers.
They study Torah
every day
as if we never left the shtetl.

I want to grab them by the shoulders
and shake,
hard.

> Can you not see opportunity
> like a trail of golden bread crumbs
> laid out before you?
> Or if you will not
> go to school,
>   let me!
> I will study hard enough
> for all of us.

revolution

After work
I walk two blocks down Allen Street
to the fish market
hurrying, hoping to find
a few that have not spoiled
in the heat of the day.
Laundry lines crisscross the street
like flags strung up
for a festival.
A dozen different languages
like so many brightly colored threads
weave through the air
around me.
I wish I could gather each one
twist it,
turn it in the light
study it.

Back home,
when I lift my three fish
from their newsprint wrappings
my eyes are caught by the headlines
of the Yiddish paper.
The revolution has finally come
to Russia.
The peasants protest against the Tsar—
they want a better life
for the working class.

If only
it were so simple.

The paper is months old
and I hear from the immigrants
flooding into the city
every day
who the peasants blamed
when their revolution failed.

They cry for freedom
they preach equality
      —just not for us.

Even in the middle
of the people's revolution
the people
vent their anger
on the Jews.

give thanks

My eyes are tired
my backside sore
from sitting for so many hours
in a single day.
I step outside
fill my lungs
like dusty bellows
      rusty
from lack of use.

These long summer days
are such a gift
when daylight waits
        even for us
before it fades into dusk.

No one bothers me
at the study tables
in the library
though the director
of the free school nods
in my direction
as she climbs the stairs
to the second floor.

I bargain with myself:
a list of English words
memorized
earns a break for my mind
    a chapter of a novel
in Russian.

The gaslights dim
five minutes before the library closes.
I gather my books
place them back on the shelves.
Every night
as I pass the checkout counter
on my way outside,
I offer my thanks
for such a place
by giving voice to a new phrase
I have learned:

It was a good night,
yes?
Tomorrow it is
a good day.

Yes,
the clerk says
with a solemn nod,
inflection
and a subtle correction,

tomorrow will be
a good day.

lull

I practice
under my breath
as I work:

yesterday was
today is
tomorrow will be

yesterday was
today is
tomorrow will be

The rhythmic battery
of the machines
                    breaks
its dogged pace.

Heads unbow,
eyes search
        for the source
of the lull.

A new girl
a young one
stands by the door to the shop
her hands clasped,
pleading.

Back to your station,
            the foreman shouts.

Please,
        she says,

I will be quick.

You can wait till lunch
for a trip to the toilet
like the rest of them.
If you can't wait, you must be ill.
If you're ill, you can go home—
just don't bother
coming back.

Her face is white
as the waists
before us,
her back erect
as she walks to her seat
struggles to feed the cloth
straight
through the machine's
hungry mouth.

Ten minutes later,
the sound of sobs
a foul smell
rise above the din.
This time
the machines do not even slow
as the foreman unlocks the door
throws the girl out.

None of us
has the heart
to watch her go.

say nothing

In Russia
it was the Christians
we had to be wary of.
Centuries
of lies
and fear
turned us somehow
into the enemy.

But here
the bosses are Jews, too.
We are their neighbors
            their nieces
            their people.
There is no reason for them
to work us so hard
to strip
our dignity from us.

I am not so good
at being a good girl.

                    In this country
                where all are free
                        to speak
                    their minds

        it is becoming difficult
                to say nothing.

tense

I	walk
you	walk
he / she / it	walks
they	walk
we	walk

yesterday I	walked
tomorrow I	will walk
today I	wish I could walk

> out of the doldrums
> the dead air
> that is this shop
> into a life where my mind
> is unmoored
> set adrift
> free to steer into the
> wild, whipping winds.

bleary

Mama leaves a plate for me
when I come home at night

she would rather wait
and have the meal together as a family
and she would rather I come straight home from work
and that I not stay until my eyes are red and bleary
and I cannot read another word.

I can stand her disapproval.
I can bear Papa's condemnation.
I can even shoulder my brothers' scorn.

What I cannot bear
is the thought of

this

only
more of this
the rest of my days.

make ready

Summer is coming to a close.
Even in this petrified forest of gray

                upon gray

                    upon gray

the bluebirds are busy
gathering bits of ribbon
and twigs
to line their nests.

They know every shop
on the Lower East Side.
They wait
      on the drainpipes
      and lintels
for a door to swing open
and swish closed
letting loose a dervish of dust
            and lint
            and thread.
They dive from their perches
tittering and
twittering;
speeding their treasures
off to hidden places.

make it right

The foreman
pinches us
touches us.
Today he grabbed Nadia's backside
when both her hands were full
carrying her finished waists
to the presser's table.
He laughed
at her protests,
her red face.

I could not
look away
anymore.

I spoke to the boss,
                    sure he would make it right.

Hardly lifting his eyes
from the ledger sheet

                he said,
        There are dozens of girls
        fresh off the boats
        who would be more than happy
        to work in your place
        without complaining.

Fired.

Just like that,
with no pay
for the week's
work.

rise and fall

Throngs of people stroll the streets
as if nothing of consequence
has happened.
Walking home in the middle of the day
the autumn sun heats the back of my head
until it pounds
in counterpoint to my footsteps
that speed
and slow
as my mind turns
and churns
and stutters to a stop.

Papa will be angry,
of course,
but he is not the one
working day in,
        day out
to keep us out of the poorhouse.

I do not know how I will find the words to tell Mama.

I make myself
put one foot
in front of the other
across the narrow tiled entry
up the creaking stairs,
gaslight catching
on the tin ceiling
reflecting its moody light back at me.
The door handle
is cold to the touch.

Mama is in the kitchen
dropping potatoes into a pot of boiling water
her face red and blotchy
her hair wet
with sweat
and clinging to her cheeks.

What is it, Clara,
         she says,
why are you not at work?

My mouth is dry
my tongue sticks
to the roof of my mouth.

A mound of potato peels
slides to the floor
as I try to explain.
Mama reaches a hand to the table
to steady herself.

But you worked
Sunday and Monday and Tuesday,
         she counts the days off on her fingers,
you should be paid
at least for that!

My shoulders rise and fall

Whatever the boss decides
is law, Mama.
There is nothing I can do.

She drops the last potato into the pot
wipes her brow

with the back of her hand
blows a breath of air
toward the ceiling.

Both hands reach out
beseeching,

> *But why, Clara,*
> *did you have to speak?*
> *It was not you*
> *who was mistreated.*

> *No, Mama,*
>   I say,
> *not today.*
> *But it has been me*
> *before.*
> *It will be me*
> *again.*
>   I take my mother's hands
>   in my own.
> *Would you have me stay silent*
> *while those around me suffer?*

>   She says,
> *If you do not stay silent*
> *you cannot work.*
> *If you do not work,*
> *how will we eat?*

It is only then
I see Marcus and Nathan
in the parlor
listening to every word,

questions
accusations
in their eyes.

at home

I work the dough with my palms.
      Thrust and lift, fold and
      thrust.

I thought things would be different here.
      Thrust and lift, fold and
      thrust.

But not for girls. Not anywhere.
      Thrust and lift, fold and
      thrust.

I move to the window
        gulp sour air
        dense with yeast.
Outside, buildings press together
like gulls fighting for a perch
on a bobbing buoy.
Clouds shuttle past the tips
of distant buildings
privy to private currents of air.

I wipe the sweat from my brow
careful not to touch anything
with my dough-scummed hands,
careful not to disturb
Nathan and Benjamin
as they bend over their books
as they mutter and pray.

A burst of hot breath,
back to the kitchen.

Thrust and lift, fold and
thrust.

wrestle

I wrestle with my own mind
and heart.

I worked for months
in that shop
day in
day out
without a single penny
for myself.
Every week,
I gave Mama all my earnings
so she could care
for the family.

I see now how this family values
my contribution:

while Mama fetches a bucket of coal from the cellar
in the backyard
        my brothers pray
while Mama washes the clothes
        my brothers study at the table
while Mama scrubs the floor
        my brothers pray
        for a second time
while Mama prepares the dinner
        my brothers memorize Torah
while Mama does her piecework
by the light of a single lamp
        my brothers pray
        for a third time.

Would it really make them
any less holy
if they cleaned a dish
beat a rug
carried the wash water to the sink
in between prayers?

Work in a garment shop
is a particular misery
my brothers will never know.
I cannot do it
only to fund such a life
anymore.

                         I wrestle with my own mind
                         and heart.

The time has come
to take
what I need
for myself.

When I find a new job
I will hold some money back
each week
for myself
for textbooks
for tuition.

not one word

I found another shop—
worse than the first,
but I have given up
my chance
to be choosy.

I know enough
this time
to keep my mouth shut
in front of the boss.

The machines punch away in the stuffy workroom

stitch, gather
stitch, gather
stitch, gather
stitch, gather

I make only four dollars a week
and I have to pay rent
for the stool
I sit upon.
But if I finish my work quickly
I can help the drapers.

The toilet is indoors
but still, we are only permitted
to use it once in the morning
and once again after lunch.
It backs up,
overflows into the workroom
at least twice a week.

There are children in this shop
Benjamin's age
sewing buttonholes
trimming threads
schlepping piecework
back and forth to the tenements.
The girls my age squint
like old women,
the hazy gaslight
the flashing needle
straining their eyes.

> *Not one word.*
> *Not a single word.*
> *Clara, you must not say*
> *one word.*

So far I have obeyed, but it helps
that the boss who lords over this dusty shop
struts like a common moorhen
                    with sprawling yellow feet
                    drab feathers
                    an ugly red nose.
When he stalks the aisles
clucking his disapproval
I see the mighty chicken of the swamp
shin-deep in muck,
ducking his head for a tasty
water skipper
or frog.

It helps,
            (when I want to scream
            when I want to march out of that shop

linking arms with every miserable
      girl inside)
it helps to imagine the moorhen's warble
burbling from his lips.

night classes

Tonight,
    heat
fills the classroom
with a drowsy haze

it feels like
the greatest struggle
of my life
just to stay awake.
I prop my eyelids open
with my fingers.

English is a willful language
stubborn
refusing to follow its own rules.

When class is over
and they let us out
onto dark sidewalks
I trace this new
curving alphabet in the air before me
as I walk,
my finger lifting and swirling
like a maestro commanding
a host of musicians.

school

A truancy officer
came to the apartment yesterday
while I was at work.

      Benjamin and Nathan,
          he said,
      must go to school.

The rest of us are too old
for the law to bother with us.

The state of New York
may have given up on me
          but I am only
getting started.

Coney Island

At lunch,
the girls talk of how
if they save their lunch money
all week,
if they eat nothing but bread
and a glass of milk
they can purchase the nickel fare
to Coney Island
when the slow season begins
and the shop closes
for a day
here and there.

In the shtetl
I loved to swim
in the streams
in the last days of summer.
I loved to watch the traveling shows
that came through town

but here
I cannot spare
the pennies.

When my education is behind me
when I am a doctor at last
then maybe I will have money
for a holiday.

tuition

The director at the free school pulls me aside
after English class

               and says,
        Every year
        the Educational Alliance asks
        for the name
        of a student worthy
        of a college scholarship.

My eyes blink like a barn owl
startled by the bright sun.

Am I dreaming?
Am I so tired
my mind
cannot tell
when I am awake?

              With a wry
              twist of her lips
              she continues,
        Of course,
        to be awarded funds
        for tuition, room and board,
        you will have to gain
        high school equivalency
        by the time the term begins next fall.

Though I have not yet
been able to make my joy
form a single word
she must see it
all the same.

Yes,
        she says,
I thought you were the right choice.

The colleges require
sixty points for admission,
more than two dozen exams.
Here is the schedule;
I'm sure
I don't need to tell you
how rigorous this time line
will be.

I take the paper
grasp her hand
in mine.

        Thank you.

exams

If I could only take the exams in Russian
I know I could pass
Philosophy
World History
Literature
Psychology
with ease

but words
which I have always loved
above all else
now stand in my way.

On the way home from work tonight
I will buy textbooks
to study for my first round of exams,
keep them
like Papa keeps the Torah
sacred
protected
revered,

and somehow
secret, too.

But I am practiced
in this sort of lie

and I have a plan:
mathematics is a universal language
a good place
to start.

Spelling is only
learning to hear the sounds correctly
and memorizing—

a perfect task
for dreary days
in the shop.

Rosh Hashanah

The high holy day begins at sundown.
I do not know why
the cutters and pressers
      [the men]
are allowed to leave early
so they can be home in time
to pray
to make way
for a new year,

while the sun goes down
and still we work.

When at last we are free to go
the street floods with women
rushing home.

I know Papa hopes this year
I will repent
give up my dreams
but he may as well ask
that I stop breathing.

I will miss the service tomorrow.
While my family blesses one another,
goes down to the water
to perform *tashlich*,
I will be at work.

But we will celebrate in our own way.
Evelina is bringing apples and honey
and Bina is baking a braid of *challah*
for us to share.

Tonight
I will salt a fish
for our little feast.

Gut yor.
Happy new year.

soon

Ours is a life of darkness and lamplight.
            We know that outside the shop
            the autumn sun shines—
            only we never see it.

I am glad
to bring a wage
home to my family
                    but

my fingers are sore
my eyes grow tired
from squinting
at tiny stitches
all day.

The whirring machines are loud
                    (**so loud**)

            my head rings
            for hours
            after I leave.

Soon,
I tell myself,
        soon
I will be in school full-time
this will all be behind me.

But I look around
at the rows and rows
of immigrant girls,
heads down
voices silent
and I wish this better life
did not come
at such a price.

inspector

I did not understand why
the foreman came running
scooped up the children
dropped them behind
a pile of crates in the back corner
tossed a stack of fabric
over their heads.

> He said,
> *A piece of cake*
> *for each of you*
> *if you don't say a word,*
> *if you stay hidden*
> *until I come back.*

I did not understand
until the man with the clipboard
and the drooping mustache
fixed in a permanent frown
strolled in with the boss.
> (who gave away more smiles
> in five minutes
> than I have ever seen
> on his face)

I watch as the inspector
checks the toilet
checks the window
checks the scrap heap
checks the door handle
> to see that it opens
> from the inside.

He scribbles notes
tears a copy from his clipboard
for the boss.

> See that these items
> are corrected
> with haste,
>   he says
>   as he walks away.

The boss looks at the list
tosses it into the stove

> Get those children
> back to work!

and he locks the door behind him.

whispers

At lunch,
the children play jacks
in the corner,
the girls chat
in between bites.

From the drapers' table
I hear a new word
whispered
with a hard edge
furtive eyes
darting to the foreman's desk:

union

I think this is a word
I need to understand.

Yom Kippur

Taking no food for the day
is not so hard.
In the course of a day
I eat very little.

> *Like a bird,*
> Mama says.

What is much harder
is looking
my sins
in the face.

> Have I hidden
> in my books
> in the name of learning
> while injustice
> spreads its roots
> in the ground beneath me?

union

It took three dictionaries
one English
one Russian
and one translating between the two
but I have found the word
I was looking for:

> *union (n):*
> *an organization of workers*
> *formed to protect the rights*
> *of its members*

We are workers.
Do we not deserve protection?
Do we not have rights
      just because we are women?

tradition

Papa has decided
because I bring home less
because Mama's piecework
has never paid more
than a pittance
it is time
for him to look for work,

outside the home
outside of shul.

Today he found it
in a humble crockery shop.

It is a new thing for him
to put aside his holy studies
during the day
to work.

We are a people
of tradition,
              new
does not come easily.

old world

Inside I am anything
but fresh off the boat.
I have been ready for this
                    possibility
all my life.

On the outside,
I know I look as if
I have one foot still
in the old world.
But I have no time
          no money
to spare
for new clothes.

In this country,
a working girl
wears a hat.

She sheds her old-world feathers
for a starched shirtwaist
an A-line skirt
a brisk gait
and a wide-brimmed hat.
She arranges feathers
scraps of fabric,
buttons on the rim
to show that she has a style
all her own

                    to say,
          I earned this
          for myself.

My head is bare
and I wonder,
can it be wrong to wish
for a frivolous thing
that cannot feed the belly
                or the mind
                or the heart
but only the fickle flights
of the spirit?

          —still, it would be nice to have a hat
                    to show the world
                    I have both feet
                    firmly planted in this
                    American soil.

luck

Luck is with me today.

Not five blocks from home,
against the brick walls
of the shops lining Grand Street
a warbler's yellow breast
catches my eye
and I follow him around a corner
into a grimy alley
streaked with filth,
lined with piles of refuse
waiting for the trash carts.

His dainty feet cling
for a moment
to the curved wire frame
of a hat form
peeking out of the heap
behind a milliner's shop.
With a
      cheep
and a flutter of wings
he is gone.

A single yellow feather
falls out of the sky
lands in my cupped hands.
I tuck it into my waistband
snatch the bent
broken tangle of wires
from the mound of thread
and tissue paper patterns,
shake it clear

hold it close
all the way home.

Tonight I sit by Mama;
we bend over our work
by the light
of a single lamp
while Papa and Marcus study
while Nathan reads
while Benjamin rolls his king marble
  a patch of bluest sky,
  lofty clouds trapped
  within an orb
  of polished glass
around and around
in his palm.

The wire mesh is frayed
and twisted
I prick my fingers
a dozen times
as I twist and wrap,
bend and press the wire into place.

I pull scraps Mama saved from her piecework
stitch them in strips around the brim
saving the biggest piece,
a delicate brown scrap of felt,
for the crown.
I wet it
stretch it
wet and gently stretch again
until it cups the frame,
as if it always planned
to take such a lofty shape.

The ugliest scraps
I sew underneath
where no one will see them
but me.
Last of all,
I tack the bright yellow feather
in the bend
where crown and brim meet.

The result is simple.
          (a little wobbly
          but it will do)

The working girl
wears a hat.
Tomorrow
my head will no longer
be bare.

traffic

I step a little lighter
on my morning walk,
the warbler's feather
dancing in the air
above my head.

There are no hooks in the workroom
for something so delicate
as a ladies' hat,
so I leave it on my head.
The foreman knocks it
to the floor twice,
yells each time I set my needle aside
to pick it up,
dust it off.
I move my hat to my lap
careful not to shift my legs
crush it under the table.

Midmorning,
when I leave my seat,
    the forewoman trailing behind me
    tapping her foot outside
    rapping at the door
    if I take too long
    in the toilet,
I set my hat carefully
on my chair
where I hope it will be safe
from the frantic traffic
of the shop.

When I return
not two minutes later

it has been knocked to the floor
trampled flat—
crown crumpled
felt torn
bright yellow feather
snapped at the quill.

dictate

The director of the free school
stops by
our evening study session
leans in
over my shoulder.

She nods her head
in approval
as I take dictation
as I take the all too round sounds;
mouth the name of each letter
as they form words on the paper before me.

    Don't forget,
        the director says to the room
        before she pivots
        out the door,
    the exams are next week.
    I advise you all
    to use every available moment
    in the coming days
    for study.

If only I could find a way
to study
in my sleep.

blood

snap

Evelina cries out
snatches her hand back
from the machine
that punched its eyed fang
through her nail.

Work stutters to a stop
as she cradles her hand to her chest
too late—
a drop of blood
blooms on the crisp
pattern piece in front of her.

The foreman crosses the room
smacks the back of her head.

> *You stupid*
> *careless girl!*
> > he shouts.
> *You will pay for that yard*
> *of cloth.*

> *I cannot,*
> > Evelina cries,
> *please—*
> *we will be on the streets*
> *if we cannot pay the rent!*

He heaves her up
and out
her stool crashes
to the floor.

The clamor in my head
doubles
even though one less machine
bangs away in the workroom.

In the morning
a new girl sits on Evelina's stool
her eyes flash this way and that—
she has that desperate
fresh off the boat
look about her.

When my eyes blur
                    return
to the work before me
it is as if blood already flows
from her fingertips
and the sticky
stain of it
is all over my hands.

greenhorn

Tonight I am missing an English class
I cannot afford to miss
but I cannot
do nothing.

The papers write about the unions
how they negotiate
with the shops for
the rights of the
                    male
                    worker
perhaps they can tell me
who defends
the rights of the
                    female
                    worker.

I walk several blocks
out of my way
in the dark
under bare tree branches in Seward Park
crisscrossing the clouds
glowing with the rising moon
casting a dome of stained glass
above my head.

The play structures
are empty
abandoned.

The lights in the offices
of the *Jewish Daily Forward*
burn long into the night.

I climb broad steps
push through a pair of carved wooden doors
into an office humming with activity.

> Excuse me,
> > I say,
> can you tell me how
> a worker can form
> a union?

I am directed up the stairs
to an open hall
where young men in flat caps
pound away
at the typewriters before them.
Cigarettes droop from their lips,
forgotten
in the flurry,
the fever-pitched
sprint
to make the night's deadline.
At the labor desk
a reporter takes the time
to lift the cigarette from his lips
tap the ashes into a tray
with dozens of stubs
bent like uprooted tree stumps.

> What you want,
> > he says,
> is the ILGWU
> at the corner of Third Avenue
> and St. Marks Place.
> Ask about a local.

He props the cigarette between his lips
pounds at the keys.

>   *They'll say no,*
>   *of course,*
>   *he raises an eyebrow*
>   *in my direction*
>   *before returning to his work*
>   *but something tells me*
>   *that won't stop you,*
>   *will it?*

My dress is shabby
my hat is gone
the skin under my eyes
stained with fatigue
 —but somehow
 I must have shed
 my greenhorn skin
 nonetheless.

temporary

I miss another English class
to attend a meeting
in a smoky union hall.
I am not the only girl
in attendance
but nearly so.

When I take my turn
to speak
it is as if all those long days
at the shop
all those years
of being told that a girl
cannot speak up
          speak out
               against a man
spill out of me
like a river
overflowing its banks.

          I say,
     We need representation.
     We are made to work
 ·   *long weeks—seventy hours*
     or more.

          I say,
     They do not allow us
     to use the restroom
     when we need it.

          I say, .
     (even though it makes a flush
     rise in my face)

They touch us
in inappropriate ways.

I say,
They lock the door
from the outside
so we cannot escape.
What if there was a fire?

I say,
There is no place for us
to hang our hats.

The men laugh at this
and use the break
in my words
to say:

We are concerned
with elevating conditions
for the working
man.

Girls are temporary workers
who could never be relied upon
to stand fast
in a long, drawn-out strike.

If you do not like your lot
perhaps you should
stay home.

Get a husband
to work for you.

Snickering
and taunts
ring in my ears.
My neck
pulses
with heat.

Temporary.
Of all their words, that is the one
that burns;
is that not exactly my plan—
to stay only as long as it takes
to pass the exams
to earn my college scholarship?

I feel a tap on my shoulder.
A girl with russet hair
and a long hawk-like nose
leans forward

                    and says,
          You know they only say that
          to make you give up
          go away
          quit pestering them.

She lifts a single eyebrow
                    as if to say,
          Well,
          did it work?

She thrusts a hand over my shoulder
and shakes mine
vigorously.

                Pauline,
                        she says
                        by way of introduction.
                Walk with me.

At the next meeting
we wear neckties over our blouses
part our hair
slick it back
in a fashion that is severe
                        serious,
                        masculine.
We settle into our seats
make ourselves comfortable,
and I say again
what I have come to say
but stronger this time
for my voice
is not alone.

talk

When I came to this country
I walked the winter sidewalks,
my breath lighting the way before me
in bright white bursts,
with only the brisk swishing of skirts
and the stamp
of thousands of boots
walking beside me
for conversation.

Now I talk
as I walk
between the vendors
      wheeling pushcarts brimming
      with a late crop of filberts,
      gourds, crates of fresh eggs
      into place,
I step over gutters
running with ice-cold water
that smells of day-old fish,
sidle up to the girls
on either side of me.

    Is there a union
    in your shop?
        I say,
    What would you ask for
    if there were?

    I am going tonight,
    to petition
    for a union of our own.

    Will you join me?

fired (again)

When the shop doors open
in the morning
all the other girls file inside.

The foreman shoves me from the lintel
shouts something in English,
spits in my face
slams the shop door.

I wipe my skin clean
with a corner of my skirt,
my head ringing
with the one word
I understood:

       union.

I feel like a sapling
torn out at the roots
just when I was beginning
to reach
toward the sky.

tar beach

If there is one good thing
about being fired
it is the chance to see
the shy winter sun.

My mind turns over the words
I will need for the exams
while I sit by the window
help Mama
with her piecework,
while Marcus studies in the parlor.

At noon,
I take my lunch
up to the tar-slicked roof.
On days like this,
with no wind
to sully
or scatter the cloth,
the roof is a quilt of blankets;
women working
a baby in the lap
a square of lace
in their hands.

I find an empty corner
close my eyes
tilt my face toward the sky.
I savor the chance to eat a hot meal
for once,
dipping hard bread into my bowl of
steaming soup.

I imagine the sun
soaking into the pores
of the skin
on my face
       filling them,
       filling me
           with light.

scratch

In the classroom
desks are planted like rows
of cold crops
awaiting the spring;
pencils scratch
      scribble

a stopwatch ticks the minutes down.

Numbers march across the page
in ordered, predictable sets.

If only all the exams
could be as easy as this.

speak

Mama and I
prepare the dinner
wash the linens
scrub the floor
and walls.

When at last
we have a break
in our work,

I walk
to the garment union headquarters,
say

what I have come to say
    over
and over
and over

again.

> We have a right
> to representation,
> same as you.

> We are workers
> we have rights,
> same as you.

I guarantee,
they will grow tired of me
before I ever stop saying
what I have come to say.

waiting

Rainwater runs,
funneling down coal-stained bricks
dripping off the eaves
in a steady stream
while I drum
my fingers
against the foggy pane.

> *It was only spelling,*
> > *I tell myself,*
> *and elementary arithmetic.*
> *I could have passed*
> *even if the exams*
> *were given in Greek.*

twenty-five

We pushed
    demanded
    insisted
and the male leadership
at the union
finally,
finally gave in.

The announcement can hardly be heard
above the whistles and shouts and stomping feet:

    We did it!

    We have a local of our own!
    The International Ladies'
    Garment Workers' Union
    Local 25.

My eyes turn to glass
relief floods out of me
prickling like electric currents
in my fingertips.

I have only been in this country two years
but quickly, I learned
you have to fight for what you want
you have to take what you need.

somersaults

I stand outside the union office
for a moment
tuck my hair
behind my ear
pinch some color
into my cheeks
while I wait for my insides
to quit
their somersaults.

When I swing through the door
I am stunned
by the lack
of noise
by the presence
of light.
          This,

this is what a workplace should be.

We look across the table at one another
seven women
six men
this small
but determined force
that would shake the very foundation
this city was built upon;
tear it down
and build it up again.

I sign my name
pay my dues

cup my membership card
as if I held a hatchling
in my hands.

Executive Board Member

This will only earn me more attention
from the bosses
when I go looking for work
at a new shop;

in this battle I never intended to join
I have officially
taken a side.

This card is my

sharp
shot

across the bow.

disorderly

If I am to represent my union
if I am to be taken seriously
I cannot dress in old-world rags
anymore.

I dip into my savings
just a little
for a shirtwaist
a smart skirt
new stockings
a hat
and a pair of boots
that fit.

I march across town
wait on the sidewalk
for the girls to be let out
of the worst shop
in the city.

I am sure
once or twice
I spot tawny wings flitting
at the edge of my sight
and out of view.

The workers take the circulars
I offer them
though it does nothing
to lift the haggard
hanging of their heads
the defeated
dim look in their eyes.

A policeman grabs me from behind
my papers flutter
to the ground.

   Let go of me!
      I shout.
   I have done nothing wrong!

   Disorderly conduct, ma'am,
     the officer says.

He hefts me up
into the shadowed maw
of a police wagon.
We lurch away
and I grip the bench
to keep from being thrown to the floor
caked in filth.
I lift my feet up onto the wood beside me
tuck my head between my knees
try to coax
my stunned breath

   back.

the beginning

After a few hours
in the dank row of jail cells
called the tombs,
the magistrate issues a stern warning
and I am released.

I thought our local
was the answer;
I thought
if I just made a place
for the girls to go
—a union to hear their grievances
to work on their behalf—
my attention
could return
to my studies

but if there is no justice here,
in the law courts
in the city jails
I am afraid
my fight
is only beginning.

I fired my warning shot
they fired theirs;

it seems
a war
has begun.

fire

1908

New Year's Eve

In America,
the new year does not begin with Rosh Hashanah,
but on the first day of January.

Last night, a giant ball of light
slid down a flagpole
atop the Times Square Building.
On the ground below
thousands of people whispered wishes
waiters served champagne,
the year 1908
emblazoned in miniature lightbulbs
on battery-powered top hats.

If I have one wish for the new year,
it is only
that I will study harder,
that I will be stronger
that the fight will never leave me,
no matter how hard it gets.

Weisen & Goldstein's

I walk uptown to West Seventeenth Street
to a modern
airy shop
with new machines
windows to the street
a locker to hang my hat.

I call myself a draper

> *My hands are small,*
> > *I say,*
> *and quick.*

> > The boss says,
> > *I pay ten dollars a week*
> > *for my drapers.*

I take a breath
to steady my fingers
as I set the pins
sculpt and shape,
make the first
decisive
cut.

poetry

In this shop
division among the workers
is carefully cultivated.

A Jewish girl sits in between
two Italian women
so the workers cannot speak
to each other.

A girl making three dollars a week
sits beside another
making three times
her wage.

At lunch,
when we are free to mingle and chat
with whomever we choose
division of another kind
emerges:

clusters of quiet conversation
form around the worktables
one for the men
one for the Italian women
one for the Jewish women
       trading recipes
       prayers asking forgiveness
          for working on Shabbos
one for the girls saving their pennies
       for tickets to the theater
          to watch Vera Komissarzhevskaya
          in one of Chekhov's plays.

I sit with the girls warming their hands by the stove
reading from a book of Ibsen's poems.

The words
keep my mind
humming
all afternoon.

the bottom line

In between lectures
on the way to union meetings
Pauline is teaching me about commerce:
    pressure
    competition
    sweat.

The links in the chain
that connect

the consumer looking
to purchase a clean white shirtwaist
    demanding
        a lower price from

the clerk in the storefront looking
to move his family to a better part of town
    demanding
        a lower price from

the owner of the garment shop looking
to put food on the table
    demanding
        a lower price from

the cotton farmer.

In the chain of exalted commerce
each link sweats the one below.

And who suffers?

The workers.

Stripped
drained
bled
dry as the barren
cotton-wasted soil.

trouble

A modern shop
comes with its own
set of troubles.

There are windows
        but they are locked.
There are new machines
        but with them
        we are expected to produce
        twice as much.

The foreman
        takes the same liberties
the boss
        expects the same long hours
the floor
        is just as littered
            just as dusty
            just as tempting
                to an open flame.

influence

While the foreman
steps out for a cigarette
I talk to the girls
at the table
with me.

        I say,
Think of all we stand to gain
if we speak with one voice.

   Have you joined the union yet?

Of course,
the Italian women understand nothing
of what I say
but I think of Isabella,
how we did not need words
to understand each other.

I hope when the time comes
it is the same
with these women;
words inconsequential
as feathers
        dropped
in midflight.

snow

The orders slowed
                    and so
for the first time all winter
I have a Sunday off.
Pauline and I wrap up
in our warmest clothes
until only our eyes
and the pink tips of our cheeks
touch the air.

We stop in a café
for a cup of mulled cider,
ride the Fifth Avenue bus
to Central Park
where the snow swells
on top of bushes
and bedrock
and petite trees
like a garden of clouds
round and white
sparkling with the laughter
of the sun.

alight

I passed my Spelling
and Mathematics exams!

I hurry after work
to the free school
to check the schedule
for the next round:
        Geography
        History
        and Trigonometry.

The thing that separates
rich from poor
in this world
is knowledge.
A person can rise up

        if she can read
        if she can think
        if she can speak.

I cannot attend
every class
every lecture
but if I share what I learn
with the girls in my shop
in between bites
during lunch

if Pauline shares
with the girls in her shop
in between bites
during lunch

it is as if we all
were there together.

I see
these lunchtime lessons
spreading like fire
skipping from one box of tinder
to the next
across the shops
through the slums
until the entire city is alight
with small
fierce-burning flames.

time

I wish I had a clock of my own
      —I do not need burnished silver
      or gilded chains—
tin would do
or brass
as long as the gears turn
as long as the hands
read true.

At lunch,
when we should have half an hour,
the foreman moves the hands
of the shop clock forward
to cut our time short.

      (we have caught him at it
      once or twice, but
      he is only cleaning the gears,
      so he says)

Before the end of the workday
he moves the hands back again
farther this time
to keep us at our workstations
even longer.

Only after the doors are unlocked
and we lift our eyes to the clock in the square
do we know for sure
we have been let out late
again.

How can we ever
prove him wrong
if we are all too poor
for a simple timepiece?

I feel like a monkey on a chain
dancing for the laughing crowds
with no way to break free.

the shrike

Today I watched a shrike
plummet through the air.
Its curved beak
clamped
onto a swallow's neck
in midflight.

The shrike's wings snapped open
he glided to perch
on the thorned tree
outside the shop.
He must not have been hungry
just then—
he thrust the swallow's body
onto a thorn,
impaling it,
saving it for later.

What student of science am I
disrupting the natural order of things
that I wanted to swat the creature away,
lift down the lifeless bird
bury her
unhindered
under a layer
of freshly turned dirt?

speedups

Without a machine
a worker can make thirty stitches
a minute.
With a machine
that number rises
to over three thousand.

But somehow
the boss is not satisfied, still
with such a pace

            fasterfasterfaster

the girls bend over their machines
like saplings driven to the ground
in a heavy snowstorm
until there are only two options:

      snap
and crash
to the ground

or

      break free
whipping through the air
to stand, quivering and tall.

mercury

There will always be a reason
to set my dreams aside:
    my family's well-being
    the workers' struggle
    my own desire to laugh
        and dance
        and skip my studies
        for a trip to the opera.

Am I really so foolish to believe
I can do more
for myself
for Mama
for the workers
if I do not?

But,

        how can I leave this fight
          flit off to college
      when so many still suffer
      when I can feel tension
       like mercury rising

         a wisp of hope
       beginning to drift
          skyward?

vote

The union brought in Yiddish
and Italian translators
a vote was cast
a strike called
to put an end to the speedups.

For the first time
since I stepped into a garment shop
three years ago
I feel as if
my work
is worthwhile.

sting

At eight o'clock
we march before the shop doors
                    —pickets—
arm in arm
chanting
while a newspaper man
scribbles notes
snaps photographs
while the boss watches,
fists on hips
deadlines soaring past.

At nine o'clock
the boss calls in new workers
                    —scabs—
women so desperate for work
they will betray
their own. Eyes down,
hiding under such tattered
and filthy *shmatas*
as they walk past our picket line,
I almost pity them.

At ten o'clock
the boss calls in thugs
                    —gorillas—
who throw us to the ground
with their meaty shoulders,
swinging fists
and kicking like street fighters.

I have no chance against the man
twice as tall

twice as wide
as me
crashing through the crowd
like a scythe
through slender shoots of wheat.

Before I know what has happened
my head smacks
against the pavement
a boot finds soft
tender spots
in my belly;
and I scream
through gritted teeth.

When they are gone,
we lift each other up
dust ourselves off
raise our signs high
sing our marching songs
until our hands stop shaking.

At eleven o'clock
the boss calls in the police
                    —coppers—
to haul us away
to jail.

It is not the things they said
the bruise on my cheek filling with blood
the gash they opened at my temple
that sting most.
It is my view of the picket line

through the barred window of the police wagon
as we are driven away:
placards litter the street
abandoned
strikers scatter
running for home
running for safety.

I see
how feeble our brave moment is—
how easily rattled
we are.

Is this our way?
Is this what centuries
of persecution
have taught us—

how to run?

locked up

I do not remember choosing
walls rimmed in filth
dank cells,
the concrete sweating
its misery.

When,
exactly,
did I choose
this?

brave

I stand at the bottom of the steps
leading up to our tenement,
gripping the rail,
one foot hovering
above the first step.

It was easier
to be brave
staring down those bullies
with their billy clubs.

My head throbs.
All I want is my bed

but when I finally
climb the stairs
to the second floor
what I get
is shouting.

    Clara!
        Mama cries

reaching a hand
to cup
my battered face.

    We cannot afford a doctor,
        Papa says.
    How can you be
    so selfish?

    It is that strike,
        says Marcus.

they were all arrested today.
They are criminals.

Papa says,
I forbid you to go back there!

Nathan closes his schoolbook,
a finger holding his place,
eyes darting to Papa
and me
and back again.
A pink stain
creeps along Benjamin's neck
to the tips of his ears.

He does not turn
to look at me.

I press a hand
against my temple
and answer calmly
as I can.

Just because they arrest us
that does not mean
we are criminals.
What is criminal
is how we are treated.

Please,
I say,

when Papa opens his mouth
to yell some more

let me sleep, Papa.
If you think I must be punished,
very well,
these bruises
have done your work
for you.

I lay my head
softly
against my pillow

Mama brings a cool cloth
gently
lays it against
the deepening bruise.

Tomorrow
when the picket line disperses,
much as I may wish
for my bed
for a hot bath
I know now
if there are bruises
or cuts
I cannot come home
until night
shares her shadows.

if

Pauline and I walk home
through dark
empty streets.

We are different, she and I
no matter how alike our ideas,
she has worked in the factories
since she was a little girl
her dreams
and this fight
are one and the same.

> I say,
> (as much to myself
> as anything)
> *If I had my choice*
> *I would be at the union offices*
> *tending to contusions*
> *stitching lacerations*
> *for the strikers beaten back*
> *from the picket line,*
> *not offering my own body*
> *as a punching bag.*

> She says,
> *But it is your voice*
> *they listen to.*

> *If you are not*
> *on the front lines*
> *when the time comes to rally*
> *the troops to battle,*
> *who will speak for us?*

I do not say out loud
that some days it seems
like only a matter of time
before I
and my dreams
are dashed to the ground
trampled under the marching feet
of the picket line.

a different life

After the morning pickets close
before we begin again
in the afternoon
I wrap a shawl around my shoulders
and ride the trolley
north, to a part of the city
where the streets are wide
and clean.

I am careful to go slowly,
stretching a hand
to the nearest brick wall
or spade-tipped fence post.

I arrive just in time
to see students in sterile lab coats
a dozen young men
two young women
mount the stairs and disappear
through the wide doors
of Cornell Medical College.

I perch on a bench across the street
for an hour, maybe two
and imagine a different life
                a different fight
for myself.

Not Christians against Jews
or Jews against Jews.
Not rich against poor
or male against female.
A battle of the mind

and deft skill
against the frailties
of the body.

I leave
with an application
tucked into my waistband.

every day

Mama begs,
Do not do this, Clara.
Go to work,
like a good girl.

seams

Sometimes I feel as if I am being pulled apart
by a seam ripper digging down,
lifting the stitches
that hold me together,
slicing them one at a time.

One stitch for Mama
        who wishes
        for a hardworking daughter.
One stitch for Papa
        who wishes
        for an obedient daughter.
One stitch for my brothers
        who cannot understand
        why everything with me
        is a fight.
One stitch for the union men
        who refuse to take us seriously.
One stitch for the girls
        toiling alongside me.
One stitch for the part of me
        drawn into the labor fight.
One stitch for the part of me
        that sees my dreams slipping
        farther from my grasp
        with every
        single
        stitch.

choose

Six months ago,
when I was given the chance
to earn a scholarship
it was no choice at all.
I threw my whole being
into my studies.

But now I carry twin desires
                within
and it seems I cannot
do either justice
if it only has
half of me.

If I give up one
will my heart forget
how to push the blood
through my veins?

If I give up the other
will my lungs forget
how to pull in air
to breathe?

ghost limb

They say it is always with you—
the limb that you have lost.
A ghost.

If I take this thing that I want
for myself,
how many thousands
of ghosts
will I have to reckon with?

smear

On the picket line,
     in the chill of winter,
     drifts of snow smear
     the words on our placards.

On the picket line,
     it is impossible not to think
     of the girls
     not on strike
     home with their families
     leaning over the stove
     bathing their skin
     in the steam
     rising from the cook pot.

On the picket line,
     a coat, two sets of stockings
     and a wool skirt
     feel like the thinnest rags
     inviting the wind
     into every unguarded
     flap of cloth.

decline

This fight will swallow me whole
but it is *my* fight.

I cannot take my escape
while so many still suffer
silently
though I doubt this chance
will ever come my way
again.

In the morning,
I will tell the director
my conscience
will not let me sit out
this fight.
I will tell her
I cannot accept
the scholarship.

But tonight,
it is as though I sit shiva
for myself
for what I might have been.

I bite into my pillow
so Mama cannot hear the sound
of my dreams
      like a surgeon's tray
      of scalpels
      syringes
      corked bottles
      and vials swirling with ether,
                       all
crashing to the floor.

Purim

Three blessings
and the reading of the *Megillah*.
We hold our noisemakers ready
and rattle them
whenever the name of Haman
the enemy
is spoken.

The little girls wrap themselves
in tablecloths
and bedsheets
taking turns playing Esther,
the queen who saved the Jews.
My brothers wrestle
        dance
           drink Papa's wine
when they think he is not looking.

It is a day of feasts
to remember the woman
who rescued our people,
a day when a father
smiles at his daughter.

But behind that smile
I see
that he sees
the daughter he wishes for,
        not me,
but the woman he prays
I will one day be.

I take the smile anyway,
and hope someday
he will see
I am brave as Esther
standing up to Haman myself
not asking any husband
to do it for me.

planning (i)

Pauline is teaching me
how to play poker.
Instead of pennies
we cannot afford to risk,
we make our wagers
from the button tin.

While we
shuffle
deal
bluff
bet
fold

we plot
plan
strategize.

I lay my cards flat
push the last of my buttons
into the pile.

All in.

you have a right

In some corners of the world
revolution
looks like peasants
fighting soldiers
or commoners
petitioning the king.

Here, revolution
is everyday people
working together
for the common good.

> *Are you a union member?*
>> I ask the girls beside me
>> as they walk to work
>> and I walk to the picket line.

> *I cannot,*
>> they say.
> *I do not want to cause trouble.*

They have so many reasons—

> *My father forbids it.*

>> *What if the boss finds out?*
>> *He would fire me.*

I need this job.

>> *My family has to eat.*

But I know these reasons,
I have wrestled them down
                          myself.

>   *You have a right,*
>   *I say,*
>   *to work in a shop with a fire escape*
>   *and an unlocked door*
>   *to the street.*
>
>   *You have a right,*
>   *I say,*
>   *to take Shabbos off.*
>
>   *You have a right,*
>   *I say,*
>   *to tell the foreman*
>   *to keep his hands to himself.*
>
>   *You are a worker,*
>   *I say,*
>   *You have rights.*

When the streets empty,
the doors to the shops close
and lock the workers inside,
I make my way back
to the union offices.

Against the dawn breaking in the sky
a kestrel
glides between the buildings

small
but fierce.

I flip through the signature cards
memorize the names.

Make no mistake—
       this is a revolution.
This morning's work earned
four more girls
to join the fight.

Joe

A young
printer's apprentice
comes to the labor meetings

      Joe
is his name.
He wears a flat cap
tilted to the side
and a wide
ready smile.
His hands are clean
though the inks have stained
his cuticles
the creases of his knuckles.

Last night
as we filed out
into the warm evening air

      I heard him say,
In Russia,
I rode my bicycle
through the streets of Minsk
smuggling revolutionary tracts
under my coat.
My family fought
even though there was little hope
for us there.

Why, then, would we not fight
twice as hard
here, where hope
has a chance
of growing wings?

He was not speaking to me
but I found my footsteps quickening
to linger
in the space
behind him.

Tonight, though he sits
on the opposite side of the room
I can feel my skin stretch
      my shoulders opening
      twisting in his direction
like a sunflower
pulled along the path of the sun.

peddling

In our shtetl,
as soon as the snows melted
and the road between towns
became passable
the season of
traveling salesmen
and gypsy caravans began.

I understand
        the pressures
        that make the girls
        want to give up
        give in.
They understand
        that my wares
        may be the only thing
        between them
        and a fiery death.

                        But sometimes I feel
                        like little more
                 than a traveling salesman
                        hawking my ideals
                            to anyone
                        who will listen.

Mama

In the shtetl
Mama and I worked together
in everything.
She may not have
                agreed
with my need
to study

                understood
my desire
to learn Russian

                condoned
my disobedience

but in the day-to-day
chores in the home
      in the store
we worked together.

When we came to this country,
she cooked and cleaned and took in piecework
to keep the household running;
I worked in the shops
to bring home an income.
We needed each other
we relied on each other.

But this strike
is something Mama
cannot abide.

To her,
when I walk out of the shop
willingly
when I forsake my income
     when there is no strike fund to pay
     for our time
     on the picket line
I forsake her trust
I forsake our family.

I have never felt such loneliness
as this morning
when I readied myself for the picket line
and Mama
turned her face away from me.

planning (ii)

shuffle
deal
bluff
bet
fold
plot
plan

The police
will not find it so easy
to beat us with their billy clubs
haul us away to jail
if we lay our fight before the silk skirts
                              the mink stoles
of society ladies searching
for a worthy cause
        to champion
for a worthy target
        for their pity.

trash

I have so much
to say.
I wish that my English
were
        sharp
as my mind.

But if we speak
it is obvious
we have not been long
in this country.

So we close our lips,
march our pickets up to Fourteenth Street
to the storefronts
where the waists
we make
are on display.
We hold our signs high
wear the best
clothes we own:
shirtwaists pressed and white,
pleated skirts,
spit-shined boots.

We dress like ladies
so they cannot call us
trash.

kestrel

She follows me, I think—
my kestrel.
For her, I walk too slowly,
so she takes the idle time
to circle on summer currents of air.

Only then do I hear her:

killy killy killy killy.

It is probably only
that my walk to the picket line
is along her hunting territory.

But I like to think
she follows me,
at least in part
for the company.

menagerie

Today I am scheduled to speak
at a ladies' club uptown
to lay out the crimes against us
to speak for all the girls
to sway the opinion
of those with the means
to help.

It is little different
than my sidewalk conversations
my soapbox exhortations
but today, I feel like an animal
on exhibit,
an exotic creature
paraded before
a marveling audience.

silence

I didn't see you at yesterday's lecture,
    Joe says
    as he makes his steps
    small and quick
    to match mine.

    No, I had English class.

He does not ask where I am going
but he walks with me
talking, as if
it were the most natural thing
in the world.

At the library
he sits across from me
a book of revolutionary poems
open before him.

      I have never known
      silence
      to feel so full.

meshuggeneh

Papa's brow is creased
his eyes dark
as drawn blood.

> *I forbid you,*
> *   he says,*
> *to attend such meetings.*
> *You will come home*
> *immediately*
> *after work.*

The banging
in my chest
is so loud
          surely
he can hear
my heart
pounding against
my ribs.

> *   I say,*
> *I have worked hard*
> *for this family*
> *but Papa,*
> *do you want me working*
> *in a firetrap?*
> *Do you want me working*
> *for a tyrant?*

> *I will bring home an income again*
> *when the work is just.*
> *Until then, I will strike*

and I will spend my evenings
as I choose.

The hiss of Mama's
indrawn breath
is sharp.

I walk out the door
before Papa's anger has time to uncoil
before Papa's hand has time to curl
into a fist.

But before I leave
I catch
a glimpse
of Benjamin's stricken face,
the rosy blooms of color
high on Nathan's cheekbones,
I hear
Marcus's coarse whisper

    meshuggeneh.

My own family
thinks I am crazy.

        How can I blame them?

      What sane person would believe
        after all we have seen
        after all we have suffered
          that this world
            will ever
             change?

blaze
1909

divide

Two months we held out
        held the line
        held our heads high.

We were so close . . .

then,
last night the bosses
hired translators
told the Italian girls
we hate them;
we strike only
to be rid of them.

No matter how we tried
to lay bare
their lie,
this morning
the Italian girls
returned to their workstations.

By day's end
our strike was broken.

It is a tactic as old
as the stars:

        divide
        and conquer.

blacklist

When a strike is over
when it is broken
most of the workers
go back to their stools
go back to their stitches
even if nothing
has changed.

But for a special few
the instigators
the ringleaders
our names go on a blacklist;
we cannot go back to work
even if we want to.

waltz

Because I have been out of work so long
Mama could not afford
the kosher butcher this week.

When I come home
long after the others have gone to bed
a plate of oily lung goulash
waits for me,
cooling on the stove.

Because I have been out of work so long
Nathan has left school
has taken a job
at a pyrography shop.

When I come home
long after the others have gone to bed
our apartment smells of sawdust
and singed wood.

    Strikers like marionettes
    dance through my dreams,
                waltzing
    through fields of orange-tipped flames.

uptown

I know I will have to give a false name
find a new shop
                soon
but I cannot stay cooped up
      like so many pigeons
      on the rooftops of this city
      waiting for a chance to fly.

If I do not speak the words
      that have been building up
      like a tower inside me
      ready to topple,
      I will last little more than a day
      in the next shop
      before they tumble out of me
      again.

I do not even have
the nickel fare
for the subway running uptown
so after I drop six more membership cards
at the union office
I walk all the way to Herald Square,
where shiny storefronts
sell the wares made
in grimy shops
in the slums.

My English is not ready
for a hearty debate
but the truth is simple.
I can speak in simple sentences.

I wait until a crowd gathers
at lunch
around the food carts
I step onto a stack of slippery dailies

        and shout,
    Do you know
    how your clothing
    is made?

    You there—

I point to a woman
wearing a white shirtwaist
tucked into an elegant skirt,
holding the hand
of a little girl
with ribbons in her hair.

    Do you know that waist was made
    by teenage girls,
    some who make
    no more than three dollars a week?

    Do you know that those shops
    hire girls
    your daughter's age
    to trim the threads
    when they should be in school?

The crowd looks from me
to the woman
to the child
to their own clothes

white
and pressed
and clean.

This corner of the street has fallen silent
I no longer have to shout.

What will you do,
I ask,
to set things right?

honest

Louis Leiserson was one of us
who moved up the ranks
until he got a shop of his own.

I hope

if I work for an honest employer
a man who respects the workers
I can bring home a wage to Mama
                              and
do my work for the union.

On my morning walk to Leiserson's
I spot a cracked cobble
in front of the bakery.

Out of the sliver of exposed dirt
a little tree
is trying to grow
no bigger than a weed
sprouting three
tear-shaped leaves
and reaching
with impossible optimism
toward the sky.

a lot to learn

I should have spent more time before,
learning English
but I could not help myself—
I was so hungry for
                ideas
I had little time for
primers
and the domestic phrases
they teach in the classes for girls.

I may not be studying for exams
anymore
but if I want my voice to be heard
by those who wield the power
I have a lot to learn, still,
of English.

If I have union meetings
                two nights a week
           lectures to attend
                three nights a week
         Shabbos
                  Friday nights
still, there is one night left
for an English class.

I practice
under my breath
as I pin and snip,

try to make my tongue
shake this thick accent
as I tuck and twist and stitch.

overtime

After work,
outside the grimy doors
of an underwear shop,
Pauline and I
press circulars
into the sweaty hands
of workers held at their stations
without compensation
long after the workday
is done.

We say,
There is power in organizing.

We say,
*You do not have to suffer
alone.*

They take the papers,
but sometimes
it seems
as if only the birds
are listening.

a gift

I have given up trying to sit
across the room
from Joe.

His particular smell
of soap
presswash
and paper
is familiar to me now.
Comforting, even.

In between the lecture
on the importance of educating
the lower class
and the one on the eradication
of child labor
he hands me
a steno pad.

> *For your words,*
>   he says.

I nod
run my fingers over the crisp
lined white pages,
tuck the book
into the breast pocket
of my coat.

My voice is strong
on the soapbox
in the union halls
but if I speak now

I fear
it will
betray me.

lies

        Mr. Leiserson says,
I respect the union
I respect the workers' rights
I only have to lay off workers
because the fashion in sleeves
has changed.

He tells us this
while he sends work to a second shop
filled with Italian girls
working in squalor
for half the pay.

Mr. Leiserson's lies
                burn
                so hot
I think
my skin will steam
with the heat of it.

uninvited

When lunch is called
and the delivery boys
fill the doorway
with their baskets of cake and pretzels
and sliced cheese sandwiches
whispers work their way
through the crowd of women
at the door

> *The men vote tonight*
> *yea or nay*
> *to go on strike.*

We are not invited.

That night
I march into their meeting.
The conversation stops
as they swivel to stare
at the girl who dares
interrupt their business.

I think,
how nice of them
to offer a space
for my words.

> *You will lose,*
>   *I say,*
> *if you try to strike*
> *on your own*
> *without us.*
> *They will break you.*

It is only by standing together
—men and women—
that we can ever hope
to outlast them.

I do not wait for their answers
I have a lecture to attend tonight.
If my words make them see reason
they can invite me
to the next meeting.

soapbox

When I step onto a milk crate
my head is still no higher
than the crowd
but my voice
          soars

like the kestrel
circling above
punctuating my
proselytizing
with her

     killy killy killy killy.

The throngs of people
pause
tilt their heads
add their voices
to mine.

If I rise onto my tiptoes

I can see Pauline
nodding

the company thugs
frowning

     Joe
listening.

planning (iii)

shuffle
deal
bluff
bet
fold
plot
plan

The men
will not find us
so easy
to dismiss
if we prove ourselves
on the picket line
beside them

day
after
day
after
day.

vote

The next night
in a hotel room hazy
with cigarette smoke
we lay out our demands
cast our votes
call for a joint strike

the whole shop
      —men and women—
will walk out together
tomorrow.

We raise our right hands
invoke King David's psalm:

>*If I turn traitor*
>*to the cause I now pledge*
>*may this hand wither*
>*from the arm I now raise.*

I clench my jaw
to keep
      from coughing the smoky air
      out of my lungs
to keep
      the stern, determined set
      of my face
      from melting into a wide
      jubilant
      smile.

red light

Mr. Leiserson knows
very well
that this fight hinges
on public opinion.

He hires detectives
sets them like leeches
on the skin
to draw out the troublemakers,
the infected blood.
He pays prostitutes
to mingle in our ranks
stir up trouble
start fights with the men
add color
to the newspaper reports.
He tells the papers
we are ungrateful
ungodly girls,
the men who strike with us
our procurers
in the oldest trade.

[If a woman is disobedient
she must be a prostitute.
If a woman wants an education
she must be a prostitute.
If a woman walks out on strike
of course
she must be a prostitute.]

It is hard enough to get the girls
to walk out in the first place.

Their families depend
on the money they bring home.
Then, when the papers
call the strikers whores
their fathers
or husbands
call them home again;
forbid them
to walk out with us.

If I ever find the time
to fall in love
I will surely choose a man
who wants a thinking wife.

dent

The bosses have sugared the police
it does not matter
if I cry out in Yiddish
        Russian
        English

only that their clubs
dent
      my flesh
      break
          my will

      crack double over   *crack crack*
           drop to my knees *crack*
           slump back,
  crack crack blinking

      blows fall like rain
      out of a perfectly blue sky.

part of me

The strike goes on without me
for a day;
the union sent me home
to rest
to gather my strength
to summon my nerve.

I wanted to say
I am fine
those gorillas did not rattle me.

But today
I do not feel like a warrior
brave
armored
fierce.

I feel like a sparrow
harrying a hawk
to save her clutch,
      a sparrow
who only just escaped
with her life.

I will be back in front of Leiserson's tomorrow
but for now, I sit by the window
watching the songbirds
flutter and soar outside, try
to let my bruises heal
my head settle,
let my worries
flap away on their wings.

Mama begs,
No more fighting.
No more picket lines.
Please, Clara,
no more.

I sigh
and say,
It is part of me, Mama.
Their suffering
out there
is part of me.

ask

I did not plan to speak so freely
but he is a fighter
he knows the toll
a long, drawn-out battle
can take.

So when
        Joe
asks how our strike is faring
how I
am holding up

my heart spills out of my lips
before I even decide
to respond

> *I never imagined*
> *it would take so long*
> *for the union men to work with us*
> *for the girls to stand up*
> *for themselves.*
>
> *Some days*
> *I am just so tired*
> *of fighting.*
>
> *Some days*
> *I want only to sit*
> *at the evening table*
> *with my family*
> *and feel no scorn*
> *no disappointment*
> *no heartbreak.*

Some days
I wish some other girl
would fight this fight
instead.

He offers no easy answer
but what a difference
it makes
to be asked.

planning (iv)

shuffle
deal
bluff
bet
fold
plot
plan

The girls
will find strength
in numbers
strength in a strike
that stretches beyond
the doors
of a single shop

starting with our own:
Triangle and Leiserson's
marching
to the same songs
at the same time
with the same voice.

Triangle

The leaves are turning
burgundy, mustard, vermilion.

When the wind blows,
      they dance like flames.

            Pauline says,
You must stop employing children.

            The bosses say,
What children?

            Pauline says,
You cannot lock the factory doors
from the outside.

            The bosses say,
The workers are thieves—
how else can we protect our inventory?

            Pauline says,
You must repair the fire escape.

            The bosses say,
Let them burn.
They are all just a bunch of cattle
anyway.

And so, today,
while I march
in front of Leiserson's,
150 workers
from the Triangle Waist Factory

march in front of the Asch Building.
The foremen sneer down
from nine stories up.

Chant and march,
march and chant
drowning out the clatter

> *stitch, gather*
> *stitch, gather*
> *stitch, gather*
> *stitch, gather*

of hundreds of machines
upstairs.

slander

When the workday ends
and the picket line closes
we hurry
heads down
shoulders hunched
against the wind,
against fallen leaves
hurled like spoiled tomatoes
against our skirts.

The door to the union office sweeps open
we are folded into blankets
ushered onto cushioned chairs.

The woman who hands me a teacup
filled and piping hot
as much to warm my hands
as anything
has the soft skin
unweathered cheeks
pitying eyes
of a fine lady
from uptown.

I take the teacup
and the pity, too.

She places a hand mirror
a delicate white kerchief
on the chair beside me.

       This will never work,
         I say

to the room
to anyone who will listen
when my mouth has thawed enough
to open and close
as it should,

a few hundred of us
on the picket lines
while so many thousands more
wait at their workstations
until their own suffering
spills over
onto the sidewalks.

What we need
is a general strike,
all the shops, together.

No one gives in
until we win.

The room erupts
into arguments.

I lift the mirror to my eyes
wipe specks of black grit
onto the pristine cloth,
wipe the day's slander
from my cheeks.

so easy

Does a bone break easier
on a cold autumn day
when leaves crunch under boot heels
and frost forms
on anything
that stands still, even for a moment?

If they strike me today,
will my bones shatter
like an icicle
falling from a rooftop
smashing against the ground?

In the summer,
I felt strong as an ox
dragging the plow behind me,
carving the way to a better life.

Now I am the chaff
left behind
covered in hoar:
brittle
exposed

so easy to break.

fresh

Worry
is getting in the way
of Joe's smile.

He notices
though I try not to wince
or whimper
if I take a wrong step
if I bump against
the fresh bruises
on my shoulders,

he notices
how much
how often
those gorillas hurt me.

I cannot stop now
so what is the point

        of saying,
    I am worried,
    too.

fists

Every night has a sound.

Some nights
it is a muted lullaby
seeping through a crack
in a street-side window
that keeps time with my steps.

Some nights
it is the papery whispers
of bat wings swooping
between buildings.

Some nights
it is the calm
quiet
of glittering stars.

Once I even heard an owl hooting—
what could an owl want
in this falling-down forest
of tenements?

But the sound of this night
is footsteps.
And not only mine.

First it was one set
stepping out from the shadows
falling in
following
behind me.

Then a second
set of footsteps,
heavier
faster
closing in.

I whip around
to face their fists
to throw my own
in return.

They do not speak

but their message is
                    painfully

            clear

                                slap scratch
                              punch pummel
                        kick kick spit

until the only sound
is footsteps running away
blood dripping
pooling
on pavement.

Gorky

I wake in a cot
at the hospital,
bandages swaddling
my head.

I turn
toward the wan light
from the single, high window
above me.
My vision is blurred,
sleep-slurred

a small
feathered
body
            stirs,
shakes its wings,
lifts off the windowsill.

After Mama and Papa have gone,

        Joe
sits on the edge of my cot.
He pulls a slim volume
from his breast pocket
and begins to read:

> Over the gray plain of the sea
> winds are gathering the storm-clouds
> Between the thunder and the sea
> proudly soars the stormy petrel,
> a streak of sable lightning

Now his wing the wave caresses,
now he rises like an arrow
cleaving clouds
and crying fiercely

I fall asleep again
tears wetting the pillow
beneath my bruised head.

visitors

Nathan comes to visit,
clears his throat once,
                              twice.
I reach out a hand
and a smile;
he takes it
sets a pair of library books
on the table beside my hospital bed
with a smile for me, too.

Benjamin trails in behind him
presses a clouded blue orb
into my palm
nestles in
beside me.

By the second week
I can sit up,
read for a few minutes
at a time,
talk a little to the reporters
who line my bedside,
practice the twist
            and flick
of thumb and wrist,
sending Benjamin's marble
rolling across
the hummocks and canyons
of the coarse hospital
blanket.

I measure my health
each day

not by the doctor's consultation
but by the breadth
of Joe's smile.

electric

The whole city is alive tonight.

Pauline wheels me to the hospital window
to a view of the sidewalks below
crammed with people
marveling
at Mr. Edison's incandescent bulbs
marching rank and file
across bridges
under arches
to the tops of towers
touching the sky.

Even a huge harvest moon
seems pale tonight.

> *Just think,*
>> Pauline says,
> *if thousands of tiny lights*
> *can outshine the moon,*
> *is there anything*
> *thousands of us*
> *cannot do?*

suffrage

The morning of my last day
in the hospital
when I wake from a nap
the foot of my bed is lined with women
who have the same
hawk's gaze
that I see in the mirror
each morning.

They did not come looking for a victim
for a charity case
they came looking for a soldier
a compatriot
a comrade.

They, who fight for votes
we, who fight for rights
may be fighting
the same battle
after all.

holiday

The union gives me light work
my first day out of the hospital.

Pauline and I sit
on a pair of cushioned chairs.
A banner stretches
between us;
we stitch one letter at a time

WE SHALL FIGHT UNTIL WE WIN

drifting gradually
to the center.

She pulls the needle
out from between her lips

and says,
When this is all over
let's take a holiday
in the country.

You can bring your Joe,
she says,
I will bring my Frieda.

We will eat grapes
and soft cheeses
nap like ladies of leisure
in meadows stitched
with wildflowers
while silly birds
with no real business at hand

twitter and flit
above us.

starve quick

My first day back
on the picket line
a reporter
asks a question
then puffs breaths into his hands
to keep them warm enough
to scratch the pencil across
his steno pad.

> *Why do you do this?*
>   *he asks.*
> *Isn't it better to make some money*
> *in the shop*
> *than to make nothing*
> *out here*
> *marching in the snow*
> *dodging insults and billy clubs?*

We keep moving
to stay warm
tossing answers
over our shoulders.

> *We will starve either way.*
> *They will harass us either way.*
> *If our only choice is to starve quick*
> *or starve slow,*
> *we choose quick.*

> *No wonder,*
>   *he says with a laugh,*
> *no wonder they call you*
> *a pint*
> *of trouble.*

together

At the end of a long day
at the union office,
a familiar
hopeful smile
beneath an off-kilter flat cap
waits for me
to walk with me
to my night class.

        Joe
has no interest
in English classes
and yet
he is here.
The gorillas may hide
around any corner
and yet
he is here.

When I am with him,
I can feel my spine
unbowing,
the weight stacked
on my slight shoulders
sloughing off.

My breath trips
my heart flips into my throat,
but I remember that word
with its bars and barbs

        [wife]

I see the same
wariness
in his eyes.
This thing
that pulls us together
frightens us both
and yet
he is here.

We walk
on cobbled streets,
updrafts of air
pulling away the space
between us
until our shoulders
brush together
with each step.

gorillas

We pace two by two
in front of the door,
huddled together
to break the freezing rain,
singing,
our breath streaming behind us
like clouds trailing behind
a steam engine:

> *As we come marching, marching*
> *we bring the greater days,*
> *the rising of the women*
> *means the rising of the race!*

I hear the footsteps coming
from a block away.

> *Stand fast, girls!*
> I shout.

That is all I can get out
before I am driven to my knees
by a fist in the gut.
I am gasping
to draw
a single
breath—
I do not even feel
the blows to my chin
and cheek
all I can think is

I

can

not

breathe

the girls are screaming
clawing at the thugs
with their bare hands.
By the time my breath returns,
the police are dragging me
toward the back of the wagon.

They throw us inside
and bolt the door.
Pauline and I reach out
clasp hands
in the darkness.

farbrente

I am little more
than five feet tall
but my will
is like leaping flames
vaulting skyward

immune to all
that would
smother me.

judgment

The Jefferson Market Courthouse
on Sixth Avenue
is a forgery of a Gothic castle;
its aristocratically sloped roofs
and grand spiraling stair
ill suited
to render justice
to those of us who toil
in the muck and muddle
of this mean life
below.

My shirtwaist is rumpled
untucked
I can feel the new scab
at my temple
opening
and I only hope
it does not bleed
down my cheek
drip
on the only thing
I have to wear
to the picket line tomorrow.

In the courtroom,
we stand
hands clasped behind our backs
chins thrust up;
defiant.

Does the magistrate
behind his hallowed bench

know the punishment that waits for me
within the walls
of my own home—
how Mama's lips
pinch together,
how Papa will not look me in the eyes
anymore?

Does he not understand
                              that
is punishment enough?

The magistrate steeples his fingers
like a man in prayer

> *You are striking*
> *against God and Nature,*
> *whose law is that*
>   *man*
> *shall earn his bread*
> *by the sweat*
> *of his brow.*
>
> *You are on strike against God!*

If you ask me,
God knows
what little bread we get
is nothing close
to what we have earned
for all that
sweat.

too much

For the first time
they hold me overnight
in jail;
I sleep on a bed of wooden slats
where at least
my skirt hangs free
of the rats that scrabble
in the corners.

In the morning, bail is paid by society ladies
sent by the union to scold our jailers
and set us free.

Outside, the sun is too bright
to open my eyes fully.
I shuffle blindly home.

One look
and the worry
drains from Mama's face.
She sets the kettle on the stove
pulls the washbasin into the bedroom
beckons me to sit
on the corner of the bed.
She unbuttons my shoes
lifts my shirt over my head
helps me step out of my skirt.

In the absence of words
her hands give voice
to the things
she cannot say
out loud.

She fills the basin
places a rag and a round of soap in my hand
before backing away
        closing the door behind her,
before the sorrow in her eyes
        can spill onto her cheeks.

Goose bumps rise on my arms and legs
as I shed the last layer
step into the water,
steam curling up my
bruised
swollen skin.

The girls have been disappearing.
Condemned to the workhouse prison
on Blackwell's Island.

Every day
I am sure
I will not come home
at all.

But for me?

Bruise
break
arrest
release

each time.

I have been here before,
felt the horror
and the relief

when they loosed their holy vengeance
on the town next to mine
              and I was free
                       to escape.

The shame is
              too much

too much.

I crouch in the bottom of the basin
quivering
my breath choking
on the steam
on the pent-up
release
of relief.

picnic

Dusk has turned to dark,
the papers
    membership cards
    banners
    picket signs
all put away for the night.
I just have time
to hurry home for a glass of milk
to keep my stomach quiet
for the night ahead.

I pull on my coat
           mittens
           hat
           scarf,
the door feels
uncommonly heavy
as I push it open
against
the biting wind.

I do not set
even a step outside
before

      Joe
ushers me back inside
out of the cold,
his flat cap
tilted to shield the wind
from his face,
his lips curling upward
as if they hope

to be given a reason
to smile.

The door slips through my fingers,
not so heavy
after all.

He holds up a hand

>   *I know*
>   *you have a meeting,*
>   he says,
>   *and I will not try to keep you.*

He lifts a basket
onto the table.

>   *But surely*
>   *you have time to eat?*

And there it is
that smile.
>   (he must have seen the

>   yes

>   on my face
>   though I had not voiced it,
>   though I am not fully
>   comfortable with how quickly
>   my whole being cries

>   yes)

Joe
lays out the food
I light a single lamp
we talk quietly
laugh a little.

For a few minutes
within a glowing bubble of light
I am just a girl
basking in the eager attentions
of a lovely
lighthearted
boy.

agitated

The orders in the shops
are piling up.

The girls are restless
agitated.

> I say,
> to Pauline
> to the executive board
> to anyone who will listen,
> *We either grasp this moment*
> *grip tight*
> *or watch it all*
> *slip*
> *through our fingers.*

no better time

The union has called a meeting tonight.
So many workers
are coming
there is not a single hall big enough
to hold us all
so we split ourselves between
Cooper Union and the Lyceum,
Beethoven and Astoria Halls.
Speakers have been scheduled
translators booked
I only hope
our pleas will not be met
with more of the same:

> wait
> have patience.

The thing is
there is no better time
for a general strike.
The shops are slammed with orders
the speedups are unbearable.
Even if the bosses bring in scabs
they will never meet their contracts
unless they negotiate with the union.

The thing is
I have already been on strike
for eleven weeks
I gave up
my dream
to fight for these girls
if they are not ready now

to fight,
then when
will they ever be?

The gorillas came for me
again
last night,
bloodied my face
broke my ribs.
      I do not know
how many more beatings
             and bruisings
                  and breakings
I can take.

My kestrel is perched
on the rim of a fluted cornice
near the Cooper Union roof.

I caught sight
of her lithe, dappled form
from half a block away
and since I could only walk slowly,
my hand pressed against my side
taking shallow
birdlike breaths,
I watch her
watching
the crash
and press
of the city below.

I wonder if her hawk's eyes
can see the puzzle pieces
fitting into place,

can see what
those of us toiling below
cannot.

Cooper Union

The seats are all taken
beneath the arches
between the pillars,
thousands of people packed
in this historic hall
where Mr. Lincoln spoke
against the tyranny
of slavery.

The crowd is a sea of hats;
the girls have come
in their armor.
They line the walls
grateful for something to lean against
after a long day
in the shops.

I wait at the back
away from the wall and its crush
of bodies.
I hold a hand against my ribs
and try
to think
of something else.

The air is stuffy
thick with desperate
hope.

A man in a suit
stands,
        speaks.
When he is done

another takes his place.
Then another
and another.

(all in English, no less)

Who do they think they are talking to?
Do they not know we have been working all day?
Do they not know what these girls risk
        just by coming here?

                Wait,

                        they say.

                Have patience.

                You ask too much—
                a general strike is dangerous.
                It would only fail.

                Wait
                until the men's union
                makes their strides
                and then
                we can fight for you.

When a common crow
has something to scold you for,
he never stops,
his cries drone on
                and on
                        and on.
After a while
        you do not even hear it anymore.

I can feel the pulse of the room around me
the girls beginning
to fray
to fade.

The man at the podium
shuffles his papers,
retreats
while another gathers himself to stand.

Before the thought
has risen to my mind
I am striding forward
shouting
though the pain in my side
makes me stumble
and sway

I will speak!

I hear my words
and the buzz of grumblings
and pleas
that come after them
but I do not listen.
I push forward—
        like wading
through knee-deep water
my skirts sucking at every step.
            Then,
as if my bruised and swollen face
earns me the right to speak,
hands reach out
help me forward,

help me up
and I am on the stage
looking out
over a sea of hats.

I gather my breath
tell myself
this is just another
soapbox.

> I say,
> *I have no further patience for talk*
> *as I am one of those who suffers*
> *from the abuses described here.*
> > *I move*
> *that we go on a general strike*

> *now.*

That is all.
So simple.
The truth often is.

For a moment,
the room is silent
as if everyone within
has paused
to draw a deep, full breath:

STRIKE!

STRIKE!

STRIKE!

STRIKE!

STRIKE!

November 23, 1909

The streets are empty
as I walk slowly from the morning pickets
in front of Leiserson's
back to the union office.
I pass a newspaper stand;
the papers warn
of a general strike spilling
out of the Lower East Side
onto the streets of Manhattan
into the conscience
of the world.

Me, the reporter casts
as a girl hero
a modern-day
Joan of Arc.

I shake my head.
I know what they did to her
and I wonder
what will I have left
when they are done with me?

And what if
only a handful of girls
are brave enough
to walk out today?

Inside the union office,
we wait,
working
hoping
that by busying our hands
our minds will somehow
quiet.

      (but it is no coincidence
      that all of us have turned
      our chairs
      to face the street)

Every eye is on the window
when the girls begin
to trickle,
      then stream,
           then flood out of the shops
and onto the street.

At the sight of them

      —tens
      of *thousands*
      of them—

my lungs
are stunned
to stillness,
my heart bangs
against my ribs
as if it would split
my chest apart.

Pauline crashes through the door

> *Do you see this?*
>   she shouts.
> *It is more than we dared*
> *to dream!*

She wraps a scarf around my neck
helps me into my coat
and onto the sidewalk.

I clamp a hand against my broken ribs
to protect them from my
            swelling
                        surging breath

to protect them from the rumbling masses
                            thundering footsteps

shaking the foundation
this city was built upon;
tearing it down
and building it back up again.

> *This is not a strike—*
>   Pauline cries,
> *it is an uprising!*

give

All my life
I have been taught
a daughter should be good,
obedient.
That is one thing
I have never been.

But I have also been taught
                              to give
without the thought
of ever getting back,
to ease the suffering of others.

That,
          I think,
          I will be doing

                    the rest of my life.

HISTORICAL NOTE

Clara Lemlich was most likely born between the years of 1886 and 1888 on the outskirts of a small shtetl in the Russian Empire, cited alternately as Gorodok, Kamenets-Podolski, or near Kishinev, in what is now Ukraine and Moldova, respectively. Clara's father was an orthodox scholar; her mother bore six children and ran a grocery store to support the family. In addition to the three brothers included in this novel, Clara had an older sister named Ella and a brother named Samuel. As with most works of historical fiction, the portrayal of relationships and interactions among family members, while drawn from primary and secondary sources and while consistent with cultural norms of the time period, is fictional.

Clara Lemlich, approximately 1910
credit: Kheel Center, Cornell University, https://www.
flickr.com/photos/kheelcenter/5279886332

Since Jewish children were not permitted to attend the local Russian school, and since Clara's deeply religious parents did not condone schooling for girls, Clara's education was an act of disobedience. She taught herself to read and write both Yiddish and Russian, earning money for her informal lessons by teaching songs, sewing buttonholes, and writing letters for her neighbors. In protest of the long-standing anti-Semitism in the region, Clara's father forbade any form of the Russian language in their home, going so far as to throw her books in the fire when she disobeyed. But education was Clara's greatest desire, and this hunger for knowledge frequently placed her at odds with her family.

The Kishinev pogrom of 1903 was one of many violent attacks against the Russian Jewish population in the late nineteenth and early twentieth centuries. Clara and her family likely lived farther from this pogrom than the novel portrays, though she would have been no stranger to violent anti-Semitism; tragically, such acts were both widespread and common. Clara's family joined the tens of thousands of Jews who fled the Russian Empire both in the wake of mass murder, the desecration of sacred objects, the destruction of property and livelihoods, and in the absence of justice from the state, hoping to find freedom from religious persecution in a new country.

Ship manifests suggest that Clara's older sister, Ella, was sent with relatives to America shortly after the Kishinev pogrom, followed a few months later by Samuel, with the remaining family departing in 1904. Clara traveled to England along with her younger brothers and parents, where they waited for several months for passage to America, and where Clara attended lectures on social theory. The family left Southampton aboard the vessel *New York* and passed through Ellis Island on December 12, 1904. Clara's father, Simon, was detained for a week before being granted admission into the United States, though in the novel it is Nathan whose fictional illness causes him to be detained. Very little is known about the Lemlich family's journey through Europe and across the Atlantic; hence, this section in the novel is largely informed by historical accounts of other travelers.

Within two weeks of her arrival in New York City, Clara was at work in a garment shop on the Lower East Side. Sweatshops in the early 1900s were terrible places to work. An employee had no protection from sexual harassment, dangerous working conditions and "mistakes" in the pay envelope or with the clock. There was no minimum wage, compensation for overtime or for injury on the job, and a worker could be fired at any time, with no notice. Access to drinking water and toilet facilities were monitored and restricted. If a worker chose to join a union in an attempt to right some of these wrongs, more often than not, she was fired, blacklisted and subsequently unable to find work.

Sweatshop workers assemble flowers in a New York City factory, 1907
credit: Photography Collection, Miriam and Ira D. Wallach Division of Art, Prints and Photographs, The New York Public Library, Astor, Lenox and Tilden Foundations

It is no wonder that someone with Clara's initiative, tenacity and intellect struggled in this environment. In her early years in the United States, Clara strove to find balance between her dream of becoming a doctor, her role in contributing to the family income and the effort to better the conditions and rights of garment workers. After staggeringly long days in the shops, she would make her way to the library or the lecture hall and stay well into the evening to absorb what education she could.

A young girl carries a bundle of coats home to be
finished in the evening, and paid by the piece
credit: photo by Lewis Wickes Hine (1874–1940), Library of Congress,
reproduction number LC-USZ62-53127

In 1906, Clara helped form and was elected to the executive board of the ILGWU Local 25. Over the years, her tactics and affiliations shifted and evolved—sometimes she jumped from shop to shop, rallying the workers in each before she was discovered and fired, and at other times she walked the picket lines for months at a time. She was repeatedly beaten by strikebreakers and policemen, jailed by magistrates and blacklisted when the strikes concluded. For reasons of pacing within the novel, Clara's experiences in several garment shops have been condensed and dates altered slightly, and her experiences in several strikes, including elements of the Uprising of the 20,000, have been spread throughout the 1907–1909 time period.

By 1909, when the idea of a general strike in the garment industry began to gain momentum, Clara's was a familiar face in the union halls, on street corner soapboxes, and at the picket line. In the novel, Pauline Newman is portrayed as Clara's closest friend and compatriot, though the players in this dramatic historical event were many, and we owe gratitude for the changes brought about by this movement to a large host of women and men from all walks of life.

In real life, Clara was offered the chance to pursue medical school by Mary Beard. She chose, instead, to finish the fight that had so consumed her.

Clara is best known for the impromptu speech she delivered in the Great Hall at Cooper Union, which incited the strike called "The Revolt of the Girls," or "The Uprising of the 20,000." It was also during this meeting that the Yiddish oath was pledged, though for reasons of story, this moment is portrayed earlier in the novel. This strike changed the way society viewed poor immigrant women, and the way unions, employers and even the US government treated women in the workforce. The strike emboldened workers, setting off a wave of protests across the United States.

The strikers were predominantly women, many of them Jewish teenagers from Eastern Europe, who walked out against the wishes of their families and despite their desperate economic conditions. They maintained the strike through a bitter winter and in the face of slander, intimidation, beatings and imprisonment. Estimates of the exact number of strikers vary greatly; by some accounts as many as 30,000 workers participated in the strike.

**Striking shirtwaist workers sell newspapers to raise awareness
of their cause and earn money for the strike fund**
credit: Kheel Center, Cornell University,
https://www.flickr.com/photos/kheelcenter/5279774588

**Female shirtwaist strikers are taken into custody
by the police at Jefferson Market Prison, 1909**
credit: Kheel Center, Cornell University,
https://www.flickr.com/photos/kheelcenter/5279773728

Some manufacturers quickly agreed to the strikers' demands, including recognition of the union, improved wages and working conditions, a fifty-two-hour workweek and a process for grievances. But other bosses held out for months before giving in. Because of Clara's public role, when the strike finally came to an end, she was blacklisted and unable to find work.

Despite all the strikers had achieved, government regulation at the time was unsuited to the task of enforcing the new workplace contracts the strikers fought so hard to win; it would take an unprecedented workplace tragedy for the collective conscience of the city to finally bring about much-needed reform. On March 25, 1911, a dropped match started a fire in the Triangle Shirtwaist Factory. New Yorkers out for a stroll in Washington Square watched helplessly from below as the fire escape broke away from the building and men and women, engulfed in flames, with no other escape left to them, threw themselves to the ground eight stories below. When the grim task of cleanup began, bodies were found piled in the elevator shaft and against locked exit doors. Nearly half of the 146 workers killed in the fire were teenagers.

When Clara and Pauline and many others spoke in the aftermath of the fire of the need for reform, the public finally listened. More than thirty laws were passed regulating working conditions and fire safety in both publicly and privately owned workplaces in New York.

Clara met Joe Shavelson in 1909. They married a few years later and together they raised three children: Charlie, Martha and Rita. Clara Lemlich Shavelson was a wife and mother and grandmother, a tireless activist and a lifelong student. She never realized her dream of attending medical school, but neither did she stop learning. To her last days, she was a passionate student of language and literature, and a lover of the arts.

Over the years, Clara's causes evolved as the tumultuous twentieth century unfolded. She worked as a suffragist, and as a factory inspector for the union. She participated in hunger marches during the Great Depression, and spoke out against fascism in the years leading up to World War II. She demonstrated for peace during the Korean War, and she even helped the orderlies to organize in the nursing home where she lived out the last years of her life.

Clara died in 1982. She leaves us with a story well worth remembering, and with a challenge: to see the suffering of others as part of ourselves, and to do something about it.

INTERVIEW

The following interview was conducted in 2014 between the author and several members of Clara's family, including her daughter Rita Margules, her daughter-in-law, Evelyn Velson, and her grandchildren Joel Schaffer, Julia Velson, Jane Margules and Adela Margules.

How did having Clara as a grandmother affect the way you saw the world when you were a teenager, and the person you have become?

Julia: I have this endless belief in the ability of people acting together to change the world. That's really the greatest legacy I have from Clara and from my dad, believing not only in the necessity of change, but in the possibility of change. When you have these kinds of role models, it's a little bit easier to believe that people acting together have tremendous power.

She was a pretty amazing woman. She was very intense, very committed to a set of ideals, very brave. She was something.

Adela: My grandmother was one of the most important people in my life as a child. I felt her unconditional love, I learned about her life's activities through her stories, I learned to love to read from her, and I loved to exercise with her in our living room. She told me I could be anything I wanted to be, and she encouraged me to explore all options, to get an education. Most important, I learned the importance of helping others who were less fortunate and in need of support.

These values, along with a commitment to social justice, equality for all and standing up for what you believe to be right are at the very core of who I am today and how I have lived my life. I have worked as the executive director of a community health center in one of the poorest and most troubled neighborhoods in the city of Boston for thirty-three years. Every day I am able to help others, ensure there is health equity and be the voice for the underserved in many settings. I am not afraid to speak my mind, and I work collaboratively with many others to ensure meaningful change at the community and individual levels. Most of the people we serve are immigrants from all over the world, just like my grandmother was.

Also, my grandmother told me it was important to find someone to share my life with, to love and be loved. I know she would be thrilled to know my wife, Bernita, and to know that we are happy together and that we share the same fundamental social values and views about the importance of family.

Joel: In college, I would always ask myself, "What is the good life? What is the just life? What is the honorable life?" Because of her strength and determination, I would always ask myself, "What would Clara do? What did she think was important? What would my family do?" So it wasn't just Clara; it was her kids, my mother, that helped me find my way when I got lost. She gave me a sense of mooring in a very difficult world.

In college, there are so many questions to answer. Who do I want to be? Where do I want to go? She made choices that seemed to be based on good values; I thought, maybe I'll use those same values. As a consequence, my life ended up being in the labor movement; I now mediate labor disputes as a commissioner with the Federal Mediation and Conciliation Service.

Just over a hundred years ago, Clara and her family immigrated to the United States. What do you think young immigrants today can learn from her story?

Adela: At a very young age, my grandmother had the courage to stand up for what she believed and the commitment to fight for what is just. A youthful voice is as relevant as a mature voice and can be heard just as loudly.

Julia: I hope that young immigrants can learn that they should stand up in the face of adversity. The only real movements for social change, certainly in the United States, and perhaps everywhere in the world, came from people like my grandmother. They came from the working people, they came from the poor people, they came from the immigrants. I would hope that young immigrants would assume that they have the same kind of rights that my grandmother believed that she had: the right to a decent wage, the right to decent working conditions, the right to not be oppressed and not be discriminated against.

If Clara were alive today, what do you think she would say about the decline of garment unions and the resurgence of sweatshops in the United States?

Jane: I think she would say we have a lot more work to do, that we always have to keep fighting; keep fighting for your rights—to get the ones you want and to keep the ones you have.

It's kind of sad how the advances of the labor movement have been eaten away at, that the owners of the corporations have found ways to undo these advances by outsourcing jobs to poorer countries, by taking advantage of workers who are not unionized. She would definitely be on the front lines, working to change that, to make sure that people were getting a fair wage, that their workplace was safe and that they had the right to organize.

Just over a hundred years after the Triangle Shirtwaist Factory fire, a garment factory collapsed in Bangladesh, claiming the lives of over one thousand women. What do you think Clara would say about our role as consumers in an international market?

Julia: The notion of globalization is not a new one. Lenin wrote about it more than a hundred years ago. I think the idea that employers would go all over the globe in search of the cheapest labor is an idea to which my grandmother would say, "Well, of course that's what they are going to do, what would you expect them to do?"

I think that her reaction would be that she would want people to understand the economics of labor, the economics of production. I think her campaign most likely would be an educational one. This is a complicated issue because obviously, yes, I would like to buy all of my clothes from locally sourced, sustainably created places—those things may or may not be available to me, and if they were available, I may or may not be able to afford them. But I think the key is still education. This goes back to the cliché: *Workers of the World, Unite.* If you want people to have adequate wages, people all over the world have to have those wages. You can't just have it in the industrialized states, because the owners of capital will just go someplace else.

Jane: She would be working here to organize consumers to support our sisters and brothers in Bangladesh who are working in these horrible conditions. She would probably organize boycotts of stores that have factories in Bangladesh, probably spearhead a program to educate people about where their clothes are manufactured and the conditions the workers are working under. I think she would be hard at work—she would have a lot to do!

I've seen clothes that are labeled organic; they have fair trade policies in coffee and the chocolate trades—why not in the garment trade?

Is there something the history books don't reveal about Clara that you feel would be important for young people to know about her life and work?

Adela: She was an incredibly loving grandmother who spent endless hours with me, my sister and my brother, looking after us while my mother and father worked. She lived simply in her apartment in Brooklyn, which had two rooms, a tiny kitchen and bathroom. The apartment was filled with books of all kinds and a candy dish waiting with sweets for us. She was really an ordinary woman who would be embarrassed at the "fame" she has garnered over the years.

She made delicious blintzes and rugelach.

Joel: She made the best rugelach you could ever believe, and I think you should include the recipe in the book. I tell you—she would make dozens and she would have to hide them from us!

Evelyn: No doubt you will also receive stories of her rugelach, which she made for all of her grandkids. This labor-intensive effort of crescent-shaped, filled cookies, each wrapped individually in paper, would be sent to the children for special occasions and upon request!

At my husband's memorial in New York City some old friends of his spoke about his family, their welcoming, open home, the books, the music, the discussions that prevailed.

Clara was a mother as well as a worker. Clara exercised. She had facial exercises and body exercises, and once, when visiting in California, she showed my then-still-young daughter how she could stand on her head! She must have been at least seventy-five at that time.

This book is about Clara's work in the garment industry, but she had many other causes and pursuits in her life. Can you speak a little bit about her other passions?

Rita: My mother was constantly out getting petitions signed for some social cause. I don't think she ever lost her ability to understand that people had to work together and bury their differences for a common cause.

Young women, whether they are twelve years old and in middle school, or whether they are sixteen years old and they are in high school, or whether they are twenty years old and they are in college, there are opportunities for them that did not exist when my mother was that age, but she struggled all her life to make sure that these opportunities did not fade away once they had become a part of the norm of life.

During the Depression, she led a bread strike because the cost of bread was so high, she led a meat strike for the same reason, she led a rent strike. She went to Washington when Hoover was the president to fight for the soldiers and the veterans. She also ran for public office in what is now the City Council.

Her entire life, I would say, was spent in social activity. My mother was one of the founders of a women's organization originally called the United Council of Working-Class Women. The name changed, but the aim was the same: that women should unite for social justice and for causes that affected women's lives and their ability to maintain their independence. Before she went out to California, to the Jewish Home for the Aged, she was out getting signatures for peace. She was remarkable that way.

Is there anything you would like us to know about Clara's later years?

Joel: She was a regular person. I think one of the dangers is thinking that people who are politically active are somehow different than us. They are just people who are a little more successful at being what we want to be. I think that's what Mandela did: he reminded us of who we wanted to be and who we could be, and I think that's what Clara offers us today. You know, you can choose to live a life of service and a life of honor and dignity without giving up your values.

It has been said that when you're politically involved, you sometimes overlook your family life and your personal life. That was to some extent true about Clara, but she also did things that made her personally happy. She enjoyed opera and the theater. She loved to cook and she did crazy exercises every day. She was always trying to balance what made her happy with her responsibility to others.

Rita: For years I shunned away from this because she was my mother. She wasn't Clara Lemlich, she was Clara Shavelson; she was my mother. It's only in recent years that I have begun to realize that while I regarded her as my mother, she was looked upon by other people, probably thousands that I never knew, as a symbol of what somebody can accomplish with sufficient determination.

She was not afraid to defy her father, who did not think Jewish girls should have an education, and she defied all the so-called customs of the day to prove a point or to make a statement that would carry women further than where they were at that particular moment. Under those circumstances, I really regard her as an inspiration to many, many people.

Until the middle of the 1960s there was almost nothing written about my mother or any other women who made contributions to what eventually became the women's revolution. I wouldn't mind if every school talked about the Triangle Fire and the Uprising of the 20,000 and all of these things as part of the history of the United States and the role of women. In much the same way as the people who suffered during the Holocaust don't want to have it forgotten, this would be an ideal thing to be taught in school.

She's still my mother. She is an idol, she really is.

She should be.

MANY THANKS TO ...

Adela Margules
Jane Margules
Rita Margules
Joel Schaffer
Evelyn Velson
Joe Velson
Julia Velson

Liza Kaplan
Michael Green
Talia Benamy
Siobhán Gallagher
Jeanine Henderson
Cindy Howle
Janet Robbins
Ryan Sullivan
and the team at Philomel Books

Ammi-Joan Paquette
and the team at EMLA

Mary Cronin
Tiffany Crowder
Tara Dairman
Kristin Derwich
Cordelia Allen Jensen
Anna Eleanor Jordan
Helen Pyne
Shelley Tanaka
Kathleen Wilson
Meg Wiviott

GLOSSARY OF TERMS
Jewish Culture and Religious Practices

challah: a braided or twisted loaf of sweet egg bread, traditionally baked to celebrate the Sabbath and holidays

daven: to recite Jewish liturgical prayers, often while rocking or swaying slightly

Esther: queen of Persia; one of the heroes of the story of Purim

farbrente: Fiery; devout; often referring to young women of the time period who were instigators of great change

gut yor: a common Yiddish greeting during Rosh Hashanah, meaning "Have a good year"

Haggadah: the text recited during the Passover seder

Haman: the villain of the story of Purim

kiddush cup: a special goblet, often a family heirloom, over which a blessing is said when the cup is filled before the Sabbath and Jewish holiday meals begin

kosher: food and the preparation methods thereof satisfying the requirements of Jewish dietary laws

matzo: unleavened bread that is traditionally served during Passover

megillah: one of several Jewish texts, the most well known of which is the Book of Esther, read during the festival of Purim

meshuggeneh: an insult; a crazy fool

Messiah: in Jewish belief, a man who will put an end to all evil in the world, rebuild the Temple, bring the exiles back to Israel and usher in the world to come

mezuzah: a parchment scroll inscribed with passages of scripture and kept within a decorated case that is affixed to the doorposts in Jewish homes

Pale of Settlement: territory belonging to the Russian Empire within which Jewish people were permitted to live

Pesach: Passover; celebrates the deliverance of the Jewish people from slavery in Egypt. The holiday also marks the beginning of spring

Purim: a holiday celebrating the Jews' rescue from a minister to the king of Persia

rabbi: a Jewish person trained in religious leadership and teaching

Rosh Hashanah: the Jewish New Year

Shabbos: the Jewish Sabbath; a day of religious observance and abstinence from work, kept from Friday at sundown to Saturday at sundown

shiva: the seven-day period of mourning after the burial of a close relative

shmata: a rag or article of clothing, especially a poorly made or ragged one

shul: synagogue; a place of study and worship

siddur: a prayer book

tashlich: a custom symbolizing casting off one's sins, performed at a river during Rosh Hashanah

Torah: the first five books of the Bible: Genesis, Exodus, Leviticus, Numbers and Deuteronomy; can also refer to the body of Jewish wisdom, teachings and scripture

The Russian Empire

anti-Semitism: hatred, hostility or discrimination against Jewish people

Gorky, Maksim (1868–1936): excerpts in translation of his poem "Song of the Storm Petrel" are quoted in the novel

Kalinka: a lighthearted Russian folk song

kalyna: *Viburnum opulus*; a bush with flat white flowers and red berries with medicinal properties and symbolic significance in Ukrainian culture

kopeck: a Russian coin

peddling: to sell goods while traveling from place to place; to promote an idea with persistence

pogrom: an organized massacre, usually pertaining to the Jews in Russia or Eastern Europe

samovar: a metal urn used for boiling water for tea

shtetl: a small town in the Pale of Settlement in which Jews were permitted to live

tsar: the emperor of Russia

yarid: the marketplace where Jews and gentiles met and inter-mingled to conduct business

The Garment Trade in New York City During the Progressive Era

draper: a garment worker constructing clothing by arranging cloth and setting pins to be stitched in place later

gorilla: strikebreakers hired by the shop owners to physically beat back the striking workers

greenhorn: a newcomer unfamiliar with local customs and procedures

milliner: a person who designs, makes and/or sells hats

piecework: pattern pieces stitched together in the home and paid for according to the amount produced.

presser: a garment worker who irons the cloth

scab: a replacement worker who is brought in while the shop's employees are on strike. Their presence in the workplace is seen as a violation of trust with their fellow workers and can prolong the strike since the shop is able to continue producing work while the employees are gone

shirtwaist: a woman's tailored blouse

speedup: an employer's demand for increased production without additional pay

strike fund: moneys collected via union dues, fund-raising, and charitable donations that pays union members, as it is able, while they are on strike.

sweatshop: a workshop where employees are paid very low wages for long hours of work under poor and often inhumane conditions

tenement: an apartment building usually located in a poor section of a city. During the Progressive Era, these buildings were run-down and rat-infested, a breeding ground for infectious diseases, and a fire hazard

union: an organization of workers formed to protect the rights of its members.

SELECTED SOURCES

Clara Lemlich Papers. TAM 577, boxes 1–4; Tamiment Library/ Robert F. Wagner Labor Archives, New York University.

Clara Lemlich Shavelson Miscellany. #6131 P. (photographs), #6131 AV. (audiovisual). Kheel Center for Labor-Management Documentation and Archives, Catherwood Library, Cornell University.

Gorky, Maksim. "Song of the Stormy Petrel." *Selected Short Stories.* Trans. Margaret Wettlin. Moscow: Progress Publishers, 1974. 278-279. Print.
Author's adaptation from Margaret Wettlin's English translation.

Orleck, Annelise. *Common Sense & a Little Fire: Women and Working-Class Politics in the United States, 1900–1965.* Chapel Hill: University of North Carolina Press, 1995. Print.

Schneiderman, Rose, and Lucy Goldthwaite. *All for One.* New York: P. S. Eriksson, 1967. Print.

Szalat, Alex, Louisette Kahane, and Ron Rotem. *Clara Lemlich: A Strike Leader's Diary.* Brooklyn, NY: First Run/Icarus Films, 2005. Film.

Von Drehle, David. *Triangle: The Fire That Changed America.* New York: Atlantic Monthly Press, 2003. Print.

Weinberg, Sydney S. *The World of Our Mothers: The Lives of Jewish Immigrant Women.* Chapel Hill: University of North Carolina Press, 1988. Print.